TAKE IT OUT
IN TRADE

TAKE IT OUT IN TRADE

WALTER WHITNEY

CUTTING EDGE

ISBN-13: 978-1-957868-93-6

Published by
Cutting Edge Books
PO Box 8212
Calabasas, CA 91372
www.cuttingedgebooks.com

PUBLISHER'S NOTE

Upon its release in 1957, *Take It Out in Trade* was immediately declared "objectionable" by the Roman Catholic Church's National Office of Decent Literature.

This prompted CBS reporter Mike Wallace, on the November 30, 1957 episode of his eponymous TV show, to hand a copy of the paperback to his guest Bennett Cerf, the witty and erudite *What's My Line* panelist and the publisher of Random House, and ask him if *Take It Out in Trade* should be banned.

Random House didn't publish the book, Ace Books did. But it was a fair question anyway. That's because Cerf was the first American publisher to release James Joyce's novel *Ulysses*, which was banned as obscene. Cerf took the battle to court … and won. So now Wallace wanted to test how far Cerf was willing to go to challenge book-banning, and the recently published *Take It Out In Trade* offered a timely example of an "objectionable" work that nobody would defend as serious literature.

Here is the exchange (which can be also be viewed on YouTube):

CERF: *I look at this, and I don't want to read it, and I wouldn't want my children to read it. I don't say that there aren't a lot of books being published that shouldn't be. I'd be a fool if I'd said that you, Mike.*

WALLACE: *Well, what I don't understand is, you don't want to read it, you certainly wouldn't read it on the air, and you don't want your children to read it, and yet you'll defend to the death, so to speak, it's right to be sold.*

CERF: You bet I will. The reason I say that is if censorship could be confined to trash like this, that would be a fine thing. But we all know from experience that when you start censorship, when you start letting the censor have his way, he doesn't stop at preventing books that are going to hurt the youth. The next thing he stops are books designed for intelligent adults. And once you let him start telling you what to read, then he starts telling you what to think and what to do.

WALLACE: Bennett, I think that you state your case quite specifically and quite eloquently.

Wallace then went on to challenge Cerf about whether the sexually-charged bestseller *Peyton Place* and Mickey Spillane's *Mike Hammer* novels were acceptable reading for adults or young people.

Clearly times have changed...

And now you can finally decide for yourself if *Take It Out in Trade,* which has been out of print for over sixty years, is irredeemable trash that will warp the minds of impressionable people...or if it's just fun, pulpy, harmless entertainment...or even, perhaps, genuine literature.

CAST OF CHARACTERS

FRAN
She offered all a man's dreams could hope for—on the installment plan.

LEROY
He bought so much on time he might not live to make the last payment.

CHUNKY
His mind made promises his body couldn't keep.

STAN
He lived high until he was laid low.

HAP
For a handsome man he made a very ugly problem.

EDNA
She just didn't have her city-sisters' know-how.

CHAPTER ONE

SHE KNEW he would be sitting there. Many times she had watched him in the Power-Trak cafeteria, and she knew his tastes in food and the men he liked to have lunch with.

At first it was difficult to spot him. He looked like all the rest of these migrant factory workers from the South: rawboned, lanky, rough-mannered, all as simple as kids. They came to the city and thought it was the golden city of their dreams, instead of just a middle-sized drab gray collection of slums and near-slums.

It was the glitter that got them—the bright new appliances and furniture and fancy clothes. These rubes had never owned this sort of property. All they ever knew were forty acres and a mule.

And they had never known a woman like Fran Brady. She was a pert, redheaded miss of about twenty-three, always ready with a saucy smile or a seductive wink. She was adaptable as a statue of clay, and as single-purposed as an aging miser.

The big lunk finally looked her way. He glanced at the space beside him; it was empty. She glanced back, and got her food quickly, then sat right next to him.

Over the hard potatoes, fried in pork fat, she could smell her perfume rising in the air, floating toward him. She knew he was aware of it, noticed the narrowing of his eyes as they undressed her full-bodied and lithe thighs. They're all the same, she thought, and turning as she made more room for him, she saw he couldn't take his eyes away.

He didn't say anything at first. He remembered how long it had been since he last was with Edna. But he remembered, too, the smell of the farm everywhere on her skin, and when he took in the redhead next to him, he compared her scent to Edna's. And he wondered just how many places this gal doused with perfume.

Her quietness in the midst of the noisy crowd of machinists made him turn to her. Her quietness and her smell and the rich, generous curves of her body gave him the fire to overcome his shyness.

"First time I see you here," Leroy said, just half-turning to her.

"Well, it's not the first time I noticed you." Her voice had a hint of a drawl and her manner was soft. Hearing her, Leroy thought that her bare skin would be soft like that.

"Notice me, you say? Hell, I'm just like all the rest of these Arkies here. Just another grinder working away to save up enough to buy a farm and go on working away for the rest of my life."

"A philosopher, too. Besides being a grinder, you're a thinker."

She laughed a little. Not nasty, Leroy thought, but friendly like she was an old friend in a teasing mood.

"Anyway, I sure did notice you, big boy. I'm only a mere woman and you're quite a man. But you probably think that's just a lot of words meaning nothing at all."

She started to reach across the table, and Leroy noticed the free, soft motion of her breasts. They jiggled as if anxious to escape the loose but revealing blouse that held them.

He glanced at them and felt the old demanding tension rise suddenly in him. His mind caught at memories of a woman's lushness, her whiteness. With an effort he forced his thoughts away, a twinge of guilt lingering. This was, after all, a public cafeteria. No place for thoughts like that. Yet his body continued to strain with those thoughts.

"You want something?" he said, his voice thick.

"The salt."

He passed it to her. Outside of the movies and the magazines, he had never seen such an exciting woman. The girls around Rock

Slide dressed in old men's jeans, no shoes. Their hair didn't shine like this woman's, and their bodies smelled of stoves and troughs and the dirt from the ground. Only in the dark, with their heavy, graceless bodies wrapped around their men, did their womanliness come through.

"If you're going to look at me like that, I'm going to have to introduce myself just to be respectable," she said. "My name is Fran Brady and I work in the payroll. That's how I know all about you, by the way. I spotted your picture in the personnel files and decided I was gonna meet you somehow. So I'll introduce you to me. You're Leroy Landers, age twenty-six, married, work as a grinder for ninety a week, been here four weeks, come from Rock Slide, Arkansas, and—"

"Hey, hold on," Leroy laughed. "Isn't there anything you don't know about me?"

"Plenty, Leroy. The rest I hope you'll tell me in person."

"Well, I was born—"

"We'll skip all that right now," she smiled. "What I mean is, why did you come up here?"

"Oh, the Power-Trak people sent buses down to the farm districts, told us about the pay and the working conditions. Lord, ninety bucks a week is more than I used to make in a month sometimes."

"Do you like it here?"

Leroy didn't answer at once. There was a lot to like at Power-Trak—the comparatively easy work, the big city nearby with the lights and the noise, and the streets where even the poor lived better than most down on the farm. But there was no friendliness here, Leroy felt. No real kin-like friendliness. You knew a man a month and then he might move away, maybe only to a different shop, and the friendship would be broken. It was the land that made things last so long and so sure and true; the land was always there feeding the people, and the people stayed. And they grew as permanent in your life as the trees that bore fruit year after year. Things died quickly, easily in the city.

"No, I guess I don't like it here much. I'm saving in a fierce way to get money enough to own my land free and clear, and maybe to get a few nice things for the house, too."

"Well, that shows that you're a real decent guy—saving for the house, I mean. But I'll bet you anything that you won't go back and stay on the farm. You'll make a new life here, you and your wife. The nice things'll be for a new house right here in the city. By the way, have you bought anything yet?"

Leroy went on eating in a somewhat distracted fashion. As he answered Fran it was almost like talking out his thoughts, the impressions he'd been storing since he left Edna and Rock Slide and a whole different kind of life. He told her about the warmth and pleasure he took from tilling the land, and about the primitive way of existence, too—no radio, no regular newspaper, shabby clothes, no washing machine or store furniture. If he could have the comforts of the city together with the happy familiarity of the farm, it would be the realization of his dream. Yes, he would like to buy nice things.

Part of the nice things and the dream was Edna. What was she doing now? he wondered. Maybe sitting on their big bed thinking about him and wanting him. He'd send for her soon as possible. It wasn't natural for a husband to be away from his woman for so long. And Fran's fresh, perfumed beauty made him miss the pleasures of a woman more and more.

"Listen, Leroy, I think I can help you if you want to buy some stuff for the house," Fran said, resting her hand lightly on his forearm. "I know some good wholesale houses, I could get a good discount on some real pretty furniture and reliable kitchen appliances. And don't worry about paying. Just a little money out of your pay each week'll take care of it. And if that doesn't turn out okay after a while, why, we can always manage to float you a loan. The main thing is to start living real nice soon."

Leroy stopped eating then. He was touched, real touched by Fran's kindness. Here he'd been thinking that all the city folks were cold and distant, and here was this almost total stranger offering him help just like that. She was sure quite a girl.

"I might take you up on that offer, Fran. I just might. Maybe next time we meet—if we do, that is—why, we can make some solid plans. Edna'll sure want a washing machine. She never did like scraping my long johns over a grater-board."

Fran laughed good-humoredly. She got up to go.

"Fine, Leroy. Fine. You'll be seeing me real soon. I think you're one helluva nice guy. No kidding. And it'll be a real pleasure helping you to get some pretty things."

Like her breasts, her rounded little behind seemed impatient and tense as it shifted provocatively with her walk. Leroy's eyes followed her as she left the room, and his hungering body remembered her for long minutes afterward.

Leroy was in kind of a pleasant daze for a while after Fran left. He sat there at the table, his big frame hunched over the cooling coffee, a lazy, warm smile coming involuntarily to his lips. He knew he *would* see her again soon.

From the next table some stray words of conversation floated toward him. Sailor Sedlak, a huge, hairy ape of a man and the bully of the crew of grinders, was holding forth his pet peeve— the influx of Arkies and Okies and other Southern workers to the factory. Quietly, determinedly, Leroy tensed his fists in his pockets, hoping nothing real vicious would be said, because if it would be said, Leroy wouldn't stop at shutting the guy's mouth with one of those fists. An especially happy chore if that fellow was Sailor Sedlak.

"…so these hillbillies, without shoes, some of 'em," Sailor went on, between wolfing down huge gulps of his spaghetti, "come up here and demand and get—*get*, mind you!—the same wages as us trained hands. And what do they do with their crap-pin' money? Why, they live it up real big and show off right in front of your face like they were as good as you. Pretty soon us city people are gonna come second to them when there's a pro-motion to hand out."

What Sailor Sedlak didn't add, because everyone there knew it well enough, was that he himself badgered, conned, bullied and sometimes blackmailed these Arkies and Okies into buying illicit pistols, fancy cars, ramshackle houses, second-hand washing machines and vacuum cleaners—and everything else he could manage a deal on—on the installment plan. The cut he got from the "caper"—a word he pulled from a private-eye story he once read—was sometimes as much as twenty percent of the selling price. And when the poor stiffs he forced into time-payment plans couldn't pay up, he'd scare them into long-term loans from which he profited with exorbi-tant interest charges.

What the voluptuous lure of a Fran Brady wouldn't accom-plish with a naïve hill country worker in the way of his shelling out hard-earned dollars for these tinny appliances and broken-down houses, the brutal muscle and sadism of a Sailor Sedlak surely would. So far Leroy had escaped both, because he kept to himself, but now he had met and felt the charm of Fran, and the harsh aggressiveness of Sailor Sedlak was near him, encroaching on his independence.

Leroy wanted to go over to Sailor and get it over with. Fight now and fight it out hard. But Sailor and his crew just glared across the table at him. The hate in their eyes was fierce, the hatred in their hearts more powerful still. Men like Leroy were strangers, and all strangers were feared. Strangers meant compe-tition and the heavy demand on them to work harder and more expertly to hold onto their jobs. Leroy was wise to the bitterness in Sailor's curses and abuse of him and his people. What Leroy did not suspect was the more insidious exploitation of Fran

Brady. Her perfume stunned his senses, the richness of her body blinded his eyes.

But soon Leroy was to know that a kiss could be as painful as a fist in his face.

Leroy left the cafeteria and went back to his machine. For a long while he did his work mechanically. His mind was fixed on Fran, on her absorbing desirability. He tried switching his thoughts to Edna, but his wife's slovenliness only made Fran seem more lovely. He realized he wanted her more than he'd ever wanted a woman before.

He was so wrapped up in his erotic fantasy that he didn't see or hear Fran as she walked down the aisle toward him. Suddenly he felt her breath behind his ear. He wasn't sure, but he just knew it was *her* breath.

He turned and looked at her. The lights played jewels on her red hair; it looked like wild blood running down on her milky shoulders. The clatter of the machines seemed hushed when she spoke.

"Look, Leroy," Fran said, taking up his lean, hard hand in hers, "I was thinking. Why don't we meet together after work tonight? If you're going to buy things, you'll need a house to put them in. The house comes first. That's essential. I know of a real beauty, and it's practically a steal for the money they're asking. What do you say?"

Leroy didn't have much choice in the way of an answer. One of her fingers brushed teasingly across the coarse palm of his hand. He could feel his ears flush in excitement.

"Sure, sure, I'll meet you out by the main gate. At six."

She grinned slyly at him and squeezed his hand. "Till later then," she said.

Lord, it was so easy it wasn't hardly any fun, she thought to herself as she went back to the payroll department. The big goof was like a teen-ager stuck on his first girl. Hadn't he ever had a woman before? Sure, he was married, she almost forgot. Well, he'd be forgetting his wife before long if she let him get too cozy with her.

That was one thing she wondered about: how far she'd have to go to set Leroy up as a sitting duck. The big thing, of course, was his bank balance. How to get that oaf to part with some coin. For a simple stiff like him she'd have to use the "sincere" approach. Get him to trust her. Get him to think he was doing it all for the little woman, but hint that when the little woman was away little old Fran would play house with him too. And if she did end up under him, well, money wasn't everything.

Sailor Sedlak would get to him if she didn't, she decided. And Leroy would fight any rough stuff Sailor would hand him. It would sour him once and for all on buying on time. He'd be a soft touch for a well-placed caress, though. Real soft.

That was the play, all right. Lead Leroy slowly on the string ... but gently.

When Fran went on her way, Leroy decided that the only thing that would cool him off would be a dunking under the cold tap in the washroom.

Sailor Sedlak, a few machines down, saw him go, and wondered if now was the time to stake his claim on Leroy, before that hot bitch Fran Brady got her hands on him and her legs around him. Sailor knew he couldn't browbeat Leroy once Fran used her sex as a weapon.

That damn Fran needed to be put in her place, too. She hovered around every guy that came up on the Power-Trak bus. Practically a regular Red Cross girl serving them coffee and doughnuts as they waited for assignments to various departments. And she knew her men. For some, she would play Big Sister; others, she would tantalize and promise.

But he had his fists. And he did all right, too. The TV guy just told him last night that a nice bundle of cash was waiting for him in the office. The new, phony raffle tickets would be printed soon, and that would be another item. He'd try and make sure that this would be an exclusive with him. The guys would go for the gamble of a raffle ticket.

Just as long as he kept knocking a few softies down in a barroom brawl or two. And kept those muscles in trim. That's what impressed them. He had big muscles and Fran had big knockers. The bigness got them; they were scared by it.

And many times the new workers didn't even have to be bullied. They came up from the farms and the hills with nothing but the clothes on their back. Their first night in town introduced them to a treasure house: radios, TV sets, fancy suits, furniture they thought existed only in movies. In the cafeteria they'd sit and talk about how they sure would like to own some of that stuff. And there were people around like Sailor Sedlak and Fran Brady only too eager to sell it to them.

But the merchandise these too trusting labor migrants bought wasn't quite what they had seen shining in the stores. Told that they were getting bargains, Sedlak sold them repossessed furniture, secondhand appliances, leases on rundown, near-condemned dwellings.

The men spent freely. Everything seemed so inexpensive. One dollar a week for a radio, two for dishes, three dollars a week for a fancy sport jacket. Then one day they woke up to the fact that they had just enough to eat and pay the rent. Their credit was exhausted, but still the payments went on relentlessly.

But Sailor Sedlak came through for them again. Conveniently, with no questions asked, he offered long-term loans. The interest was almost twice as much—sometimes more than that—as was legal, but these new workers didn't know the laws. When they didn't pay up, Sailor Sedlak had the fun of bashing their brains in and then getting the furniture and clothes and everything else back. And then the money-making went on all over again.

Both Sailor and Fran had spotted Leroy as a prime source of profit early in the game: he saved; he was awed by the luxury of city life; he wanted to better himself. Most of all, he was a decent guy. That meant he trusted. And the way Sailor figured it, Leroy'd put as much trust in a pal as he would a skirt. The thing was to get to him first. Be a pal—Sailor would try that first—and if that didn't work... Well, a good beating would make Leroy see the value of getting a little of that money out into the economy.

It was almost patriotic. That's what it was, thought Sailor Sedlak as he got up to follow Leroy into the washroom. But it was a grim joke, even Sailor knew that. And he didn't smile; he just bunched his fists tightly.

The washroom was decorated with posters urging the purchase of savings bonds, and some free-form pornographic drawings. Some stragglers, goofing off, were loafing around, waiting for the quitting whistle. The majority of them were red-necked toughs who did just enough work to please the foreman.

Leroy soaked his head beneath the faucet. His forehead seemed to come awake, but the rest of his body still suffered from his thoughts of Fran.

When he reached for a paper towel, he found that it came from the hands of Sailor Sedlak.

"Hi," Sailor said, trying to make his voice as casual as possible. "What's the redheaded broad trying to sell you? And whatever it is—take my advice—don't buy it!"

"I don't see as that rightly concerns you, Sailor," Leroy said quietly, his eyes level and unblinking.

Sailor forced himself to grin. "Now listen, buddy-boy, I'm just trying to put you right, be a pal. That dame's gypped nearly the whole shop selling 'em crummy merchandise. Lemme see, she's probably trying to sell you a used car, isn't she? Well, what the hell does a broad know about a car? You tell me!"

Leroy threw the used towel into the container and began to comb his hair. In the mirror he noticed that Sailor had moved just behind him.

"I tell you this, Sailor, whatever she does is none of your unholy business."

Sailor had made his play at being a pal. It was only a one-round play, but Sailor was always impatient to get on to the main event. He rumbled deep in his chest and reached toward Leroy suddenly. Leroy swerved out of his grasp.

"Oh, a wise hillbillly, huh? A guy tries to be a pal and you shove it back in his face. Okay."

"Yeah, Sailor. Okay it is. I don't need help from you. You ain't even fit to discuss Fran unless you wash your mouth out first."

A crowd began to gather. Some old hands, young apprentices, even a foreman or two. They had seen this show before—Sailor goading a hillbilly into a fight, and they wanted a little action. It would be something to talk about tonight. And they were wondering if one of these days Sailor would meet his match and get his ashes hauled once and for all. They were wondering and they were hoping, because any one of them could be his next victim. With a little liquor or boredom, Sailor could work up a bloodthirsty grudge.

"I suppose that broad—oh, excuse me, sir, I mean Miss Fran Brady—was talking about me. That's the only way that slut can make a sale, by bum-rappin' her competition."

"Look, Sailor, get this and get this once and for all. Miss Brady hasn't offered to sell me anything, and if she does it's sure as hell none of your butt-in."

"Just give her time, that's all, hillbilly-boy. And when she makes a pitch as big as a Sears Roebuck catalogue, ask her if there's anything she's got that ain't for sale. Because if there isn't she's probably just renting it out elsewhere!"

Leroy sucked in his breath hard at Sailor's last ugly crack. The crowd shuffled expectantly.

"Okay, crud," Leroy drawled in a voice that was soft with hate. "You said it all that time. And I'd start taking off that jacket, 'cause you're gonna get a little, maybe a lot of blood all over it. *Your* blood, Sailor."

Suddenly Sailor felt he had gone too far. His aim had been to see how close Fran had gotten to Leroy. And Leroy's fist-fightin' defense had convinced Sailor that he was now, for sure, a Brady customer.

But now his own position had been threatened. There would be other guys to push hard, and he had to continue being known as a pusher. Leroy wanted blood, but Sailor didn't want to fight now. The crowd in the washroom weren't his buddies. Sailor needed a crowd of his lackeys around him to shout him on, to watch and remember his strength.

"Not here, mister," Sailor said, still growling, still keeping his face set and stem. "You don't know who you're tangling with. But you'll know soon enough. I'll meet you any place any time."

"The hell I don't know who I'm scrapping with. The only reason you don't want to fight me is because you know I can knock the daylights out of you, and maybe, too, 'cause I'm not half-loaded with booze. But I'll take you up on it whenever you want. Don't worry about that, sailor boy."

A burly, uniformed factory cop came into the washroom then. It was quitting time. The crowd, feeling a little cheated, filed slowly out.

"All right, champs, break it up, and break it up now! Go on home and fight it out over beers."

"Okay, okay," Sailor grunted, feigning reluctance to leave. "I'll git now, but I'll be hunting for that sonofabitch hillbilly."

Leroy stood waiting as Sailor walked to the door. He had wanted to get the bastard under his fists, but he could wait. He would wait with pleasure, knowing he would win.

At the door, Sailor sneered at Leroy, then shouted, "Just one more word of free advice, you side-meat terror. If you're on the make for Fran, forget it. Because if I don't bash your birdbrains in, her old man'll do it as soon as he gets out of the pen. And that's for sure!"

Sailor's words hit Leroy like a knockout punch. Fran married? To a criminal? When the shock began to wear off, Leroy remembered that he too was married. Only it didn't seem as if he was. The fact that he could forget that he was married, even for a second, after being away from Edna for only a month, shook him up all over again.

But it was for Edna that he planned to buy all these expensive bits of merchandise. It was for Edna that he and Fran were going to look at a house this evening. Or was it?

And what did he want a house in the city for anyway? His original intention was to save to buy a small farm that he could own free and clear.

Fran. His buying and sudden change in plans were for Fran. Until this afternoon he had never met her, never even heard of her, and now he was remaking his whole way of life. Why? What for?

Leroy wasn't a thinking sort of man, not a "deep 'un," as the men around the farm would call an introspective man. But it didn't take much thought to realize what had happened.

He wanted Fran. She had struck a note in him he couldn't shake off, and he had to go along with her, no matter where it led. He just couldn't break this off now, not with the fresh womanly smell of her in his nostrils and the white softness of her in his eyes.

Thought came to him of Edna, grubby and flabby, smelling of the barn and the earth, never trying to make herself look better for him, and not in a long time at all exciting in bed.

No, Fran was something entirely different, what he needed...had to have. He'd buy anything she wanted, because just as soon as possible—no, maybe not a divorce. But he'd buy anything she asked for, anyway. It would bring them together more and more often, and then he would give them to her as gifts. Such luxuries as you could buy in a city store were too good for Edna. She'd be a pig in dirty clothes even with a washing machine.

Goddamit, Leroy thought, why did he have to be married! Maybe it would be impossible to be with Fran because of it.

And then it hit him full force—Fran, too, was married. To a guy in stir. When he would come out he would go right for Fran. Would she want him back? What kind of a guy was he?

His own problems were drowned in a rush of frightening, frustrating pictures of Fran and this nameless, faceless man doing all the things together that a man and woman did together in bed.

Leroy's tall, angular frame began to shake with an uncontrollably trembling rage. Again and again he smashed his fists in impotent fury against the shiny porcelain of the sinks.

The quitting whistle sounding shrilly broke him out of this almost hypnotic explosion of blazing hate and self-torture.

Holding his bruised fists against his forehead, he leaned his tired body against the washroom wall, waiting until reason and strength returned.

Then, glancing quickly at the mirror to set his face in a strained smile, he walked stiffly from the room.

When he got outside the gate he saw Fran immediately, and he began to run. For a moment he felt like a happy boy. It was the moment she smiled at him.

She had been practicing that smile for some time and she was very, very sure of its effect on Leroy.

Because before she could have the fun of taking candy from a baby, she had to make sure the baby tasted that candy.

CHAPTER TWO

"I HEAR you had a run-in with Sailor today," Fran said, averting her eyes teasingly from Leroy's relentless gaze of desire. She was a little frightened and challenged by the intensity of his look. All at once it made her want to give herself to him soon, and then, perversely, to hold herself tauntingly away from him—because he wanted her so completely. To deny him would be to spite him, hurt him, and perhaps enrage his thwarted need for her even more. The complexity of her emotions surprised Fran. She had always thought of herself as a girl who knew what she wanted, why she wanted it, and, above all, the fastest, most satisfying way to get it.

"Yeah, he was throwing his weight around in the washroom." Leroy was embarrassed to even remember Sailor's coarse accusations against Fran. His face flushed.

"Well, I guess he tried to destroy my good name. That's to be expected."

She led Leroy to the bus stop. They walked slowly, and Fran made sure that every couple of steps she would rub her hips against Leroy.

"He's a crud. A real crud. I'm gonna knock his brains out next time he says anything like that about you."

"Well, I do go in for a little extra earning, Leroy," Fran said quietly, as if it were something she didn't quite like to talk about. "After all, I've got an old mother to support. I know that sounds corny as hell, but it's true. And the couple of dollars I make in commission giving one of you guys a good deal on a piece of furniture or a house—"

"Yeah, I know, Fran." Leroy said it abruptly.

"What do you mean you 'know'? You sound like you believe those terrible lies Sailor made up."

Fran had an irresistible compulsion to test his loyalty now. The shrewd thing to do now, she thought, would be not to go with him to look for a house. Let him simmer and suffer a bit. Make him see she wasn't so blood-hungry for a buck—that it was out of deep affection that she was going to all this trouble. Stir him up a bit. Her kicks would come when he would be hurt and frustrated again in his hoping to get close to her.

She stopped short in her tracks and announced that she wasn't going to take the bus with him at all, but that she was going straight home.

"What's got into you, Fran?" Leroy asked, peeved, as though he had suddenly stubbed his toe on his dream. "I just said it so sharp because I didn't want us to talk about it anymore. Of course, I don't believe that kind of dirty mouth talk. I—"

"Yes, you do, Leroy Landers. You're probably wondering why I suddenly got so friendly with you. A good buck in it for her—that's what you're thinking."

"Fran, let's go see the house. Then we can sit down and talk and get to know one another. It—"

"Hah, that does it. Whoever said you hill boys weren't shrewd was crazy himself. 'Get to know one another.' I like that. Probably you believed Sailor when he said I was an easy lay, too."

"Stop talking like that, Fran!" Leroy almost shouted. "You gone crazy or somethin'? Now let's get going. C'mon."

Fran didn't move. It was like teasing a man when you were with him on a couch or in a parked, closed car. You acted and you smiled and you played around until he was half-crazy and then you just upped and went your way, leaving him to splutter and choke like a crazed bull or an angry boy, depending on how much of a man he was. There was only one man who didn't sit back and take it. That was her husband, Stan. And Stan was far away and behind bars. One night Fran had brought Stan's blood to a boil, fingering him behind his ears, not kissing him but instead blowing her warm breath over his ready lips. Then she tried to up and go. He didn't slap her or curse or shout. He just picked her up and carried her to the back seat and raped her.

And she loved it, being taken that way, hard and swift as if time had run out for them both and this was the last bit of energy in their bodies.

But on a public street Leroy couldn't think of doing any such thing. And Fran knew he wouldn't. He wasn't that much aroused or involved. But after her teasing and refusing tonight—

"Don't push, Leroy. I'm not one of your two-buck whores."

"Fran, Fran, please ..."

"Oh, shut up and go back to your pigsty in the hills. I'm going home, and I'm going without you."

As though on cue, the bus came to the corner. Fran jumped up into it as soon as the doors opened, leaving Leroy standing in bewildered anger. She noticed that he couldn't be too angry, because he tried again to speak to her as the bus pulled away.

He'd keep until she was ready for her next move, Fran decided as she settled herself on the bus. And he'd be like a well-tamed kennel dog. Another long, deep look from her and the promise of a kiss, and he'd be fired up to good working order. Fran was satisfied, thoroughly relaxed. She felt as if she had won a competition in a grueling game. If she played a little dirty—well, she never said she was playing cricket.

There was no need to look at the street signs to determine how close the bus was to her home. When she got near walking distance, the character of the crowds changed. Men and women of Slavic background came on, dressed poorly, few of them speaking English.

An odor of poverty as sharp and distasteful as the exhaust fumes filled the bus. Fran thought of homes full of cheap, unpainted furniture, tables set with warmed-over leftovers, clothes patched and dyed and re-patched again. This was the home she was going to, the home she was so eager to escape.

That was the reason for her craft and cunning and conniving. Money. Money to buy herself decent clothes and start a new life away from this dingy quarter of a huge, sooty, overcrowded city. And money meant being free from Stan. Soon Stan himself would be free, and he'd be after her. Fran didn't want him back. Her days as a young, impressionable girl were over. She didn't want Stan's brutish, cruel virility. But to get away, for good, would mean that she would have to be financially independent. And to save herself she would attack anybody. It was her motto and her way of life. Stick to it as a way of life and she'd never have to travel for long in a rotten bus like this going to a slum that spread each year like an oozing swamp.

She came to her corner, deep in the section. In strong disgust she closed her eyes. All around her were laboring people, and she hated, was depressed by, the sight of them. If it wouldn't have drawn attention to her, she would have put her hands to her nose; their desperate, dirty poorness almost made her retch.

When she left the bus the street lights winked on, giving a dust gray overcast to the gritty houses. A few huddled people walked past her. Like rats, she thought, and a rickety house was their hole.

Her heels clicked across the broken pavements. On her left was an abandoned junk yard. A dangerous place for a woman to be near. Last month a degenerate attacked a ten-year-old girl there. She crossed the street and walked along in front of grimy, dimly lit hovels. A straggly tree attempted to lift itself out of the garbage-strewn asphalt.

The hulk Fran headed for sat squat at the end of the street, a savage symbol of the rotting squalor everywhere around her.

Plate-glass windows were covered with dingy, stained curtains, discolored and dusty. A blue enamelled sign swayed tipsily on one hinge over the door. The faded letters half-spelled out CRESCENT BEER, a defeated reminder that a saloon had once operated there.

An outside stairway, decaying and creaky, enclosed with imitation brick siding, slanted up the left side of the building. Between the circus and political posters plastered on its surface, four-letter obscenities were splashed in fireman's red. The entrance from the stairway could be gained either from the sidewalk or from the labyrinth of pathways threading among the rusted skeletons of autos flanking the structure. A second rickety, little-used open stairway braced the rear of the building. The only structure on that side of the block, it rose above the auto graveyard like the rusting skeleton of an ancient building.

For several years the building had been utilized as a rooming house, with Fran's widowed mother, Sophie, its superintendent. Its one-time saloon was partitioned off into an apartment where the landlady made her home and office. On the upper floor were rented bedrooms, dark, airless cubbyholes, always in demand by slatternly people who seemed to match its skidrow quality of filth and decay.

Tired, Fran dragged herself up the creaking front steps and entered. The foyer was murky and thick with the smell of boiling cabbage. A familiar voice screeched out a welcome.

"C'mon in, Fran," Sophie said, suddenly appearing in the doorway of the parlor room. "Eat yet? Coffee's on. Me and Renie was just havin' a cup of coffee."

There were nearly three hundred pounds to Sophie, and they were squashed, stuffed and dumped into a food-spotted tent of a housedress that hadn't seen soap or drycleaning since the day it was first stitched together. From every pore Sophie reeked of beer; it made Fran a bit dizzy just to come close to her.

Her breasts were shapeless, flabby sacks of pendulous flesh. Fran shuddered at the thought that she too, if she let herself go, could someday look like this rotting hulk of female flesh. She stared at the hastily smeared rouge on her mother's sweaty, powder-caked face, and laughed. Even this old wreck of a woman still tried to look pretty. Had to give the old bag credit.

"Sure, Ma, sure I'll come in for a cup of coffee. Even if Renie is still here."

In a rare burst of affection, Fran linked her arm in her mother's and together they went into the parlor.

Against one of the walls, on a mess of cushions and half-exposed springs that used to be called a sofa, was plumped a thin, overly made-up slattern. This was Renie, Sophie's best friend, a fortune teller who told the men who visited her bedroom what they wanted, and then proceeded to give them what they wanted.

Renie, too, inspired loathing in Fran. In her she saw her own desperate fate if she couldn't manage to put enough by now—by hook or crook—as the saying goes. Forever stuck in this gritty slum, selling herself to drunken porters and street laborers for a dollar or two a lay—when she could get it.

The two women, one hideous and grotesquely fat, the other a scrounging stick of a whore without even enough meat on her for a man really to get excited about, frightened Fran.

Fran sat down, kicked off her smart brown-and-white spectator pumps, and slowly, sensually stretched her nyloned legs in a long, relaxing stretch.

Sophie fussed with the coffee. "Awful hot, honey. Why don't you hop into a tub?"

Fran closed her eyes, rested against the chair with her head thrown back.

Renie stared at her and said nothing. Whenever she saw Fran, hate welled up in her like an almost uncontrollable nausea. Once she had seen Fran step from her shower and had stood transfixed as the young girl dried and powdered herself. Renie fiercely envied Fran's lush, voluptuous body. A cold bitch like Fran was blessed with the equipment to give such pleasure to a man. What *she* could do with a body like that! Fran—Renie despised her for having the heart of a whore without the feelings of a woman.

Fran became aware that the beer scent in the room was close to her. That meant her mother was near her. Lazily she opened her eyes.

"I just wanted to tell you, hon, what a swell reading Renie gave me today."

"Don't tell me, Ma. They're all the same."

"Excuse me for breathing the same air as you, Your Serene Grace," Renie said, quickly getting to her feet. "I'm expecting a gentleman for a reading soon and I will go now to prepare."

She wrapped her faded kimono about her scrawny body and, with a glance of sharp contempt at the curve of Fran's shapely thighs, she strutted from the room.

"Aw, Ma, why don't you run that two-bit whore off the place? She's lowering the real estate values."

"That is definitely unkind, Fran. Renie is a truly gifted fortune teller. A little too gifted, to tell the real truth. Lately, all she's been giving me is a bad reading, every day another bad reading."

"She's probably making so much money laying old Chunky's customers that soon she'll buy this place and throw you out. Just mark my words, Ma."

"Now Fran, you're just itching for a fracas. Get out to that kitchen and fill up with some food. I don't get no sympathy from you, anyhow. You don't even ask what kind of bad trouble Renie is predicting."

"Oh, screw it, Ma. Don't start that crap again, will you? I got a headache. Christi I spend one damn night in the house and there's a fight. When Trouble comes knocking at the door, in person, then I'll believe old Renie."

Fran went to pour another cup from the pot and accidentally brushed against the boiling hot lip of the percolator.

"That bitch of a coffee pot!"

But suddenly she dropped her voice to a whisper. Footsteps approached, and then there was a quiet tapping at the door.

"C'mon in," Sophie bawled, making no effort to rise.

A short, thick-set man in his late fifties entered. It was Chunky Eaton, one of Sophie's steady tenants. His face was like a slab of red meat. A mustache, heavy and formless, streaked with white and rust, centered itself clumsily on his face. Winter and summer he wore a suit of shiny blue serge, spotted with grease stains, and old-fashioned collarless shirts. His exposed neck was ringed with unwashed wrinkles. Sometimes coarse, iron-gray chest hair bristled against his slack-skinned, slackly muscled chest. He was a man who was heading quickly into old age, and the dread of his uncontrollably rapid journey told on his tense, anxious face.

"Howdy, ladies. Here's your rent, Sophie."

His voice was heavy with congested phlegm. Fran had the disgusting vision of blobs of it being spat out into the air as he spoke. She edged away from him. A man shouldn't get to look like that—ever, she thought. They should always be tall and straight and strong-looking, with the hair crinkling black on their chests.

Chunky glanced quickly at her, admiration clear in his eyes. Then he glanced at the table.

"Have a cup, Chunky," Sophie said as she stuffed the rent money into the cleavage of her breasts.

"Don't mind if I do, Sophie. Nice of you to ask." He took the cup and turned to Fran. "How've you been, Fran? You sure ain't around much anymore."

His yellow, rheumy eyes glanced slowly and hungrily over her curves. Involuntarily his tongue slipped and slid between his teeth.

Fran shivered, despite the heat of the night, and for once was not pleased with her beauty when she saw the desire it stirred in him.

"I got some nice merchandise you might like to handle, Fran. Give you a nice cut, too. I always do, don't I?"

Once Chunky had been the owner of the auto-wrecking yard next door. But as he aged he turned to a more relaxing, more profitable occupation. He had always had connections among the drifters and third-raters in the underworld, and soon he became known as a fence for every sneak thief and cheap operator in the country. His office was his rathole bedroom in Sophie's boarding house. But where his "bank" was, nobody knew. And one who wanted to know even more than most was Fran.

She had seen the thieves come to Chunky late at night, and heard them depart through the auto yard and the alleys. He was always home when they came. His only "going out" was confined to a nightly short walk around the block, weather permitting.

Chunky was known to distrust banks. And Fran had seen him produce certain large sums of money quickly. That meant a really huge sum must be stashed somewhere close at hand.

Fran had thought about its location for a long time. One night she'd made a solemn vow to herself that she would find that money, no matter what she had to do to get it.

"I mean it, Fran," Chunky said again, interrupting her fantasy of greed. "I got some nice diamond rings."

"Drop dead, you crumb!" Fran shouted as she rose to leave the room.

The nastier she was to him, Fran reasoned, the less he'd suspect that she was constantly thinking about his hidden money. He made her sick to her stomach, anyway, so it wasn't really play-acting.

"What's got into her?" Chunky asked Sophie. Under the harsh, naked bulb they looked like two murderous conspirators in a horror movie. The house creaked with Fran's weight on the stairs.

"Aw, don't mind that dame. She's scared green 'cause any day now that animal of a husband of hers, Stan, is gonna be sprung from the can. An' she wants to be away from here when he does leave jail. She needs money, Chunky, needs money so bad that I'm half-afraid some time that she's gonna go out and kill for it."

At the mention of money, Chunky caught his breath sharply. He pretended not to have heard Sophie's last remark, but he had often wondered, lying alone in his broken-down, grimy-sheeted bed, just how much Fran really did want money? How much she would do to "earn" the hundred dollars he would gladly offer her? Just how much? For a moment he permitted himself the ecstasy of daydreaming about her in lurid detail, but the droning, screechy voice of Sophie went on and on.

" …and this bastard Stan used to beat her somethin' awful. He'd want her four, five times a night, and when she complained she was tired or sick, he'd whack her almost unconscious and then force himself on her. Oh, that poor kid, she—"

"When is he coming out?"

"About a year'n a half. Maybe less if he gets time off for good behavior, which he won't if I know Stan Brady."

"Fran writin' to him?"

"Not since he got sent up the last time. She stuck by him through the reefers and highjackin' trucks, but when he shot that A & P manager in a stickup, she was through. Why, the cops made it almost as hot for her as they did for him."

"And now she wants to blow town, right?"

A plan, a definite scheme of things, was starting to take shape in Chunky's junk-heap mind. Slowly he swished the few remaining drops of coffee around in the cup.

"Boy, that's for sure, Chunky. One of Stan's friends who just got out of stir, came around and told Fran that Stan was real gut-angry at her for not sending him money and for not spending enough in the first place to hire him a decent lawyer."

"Well, why don't she get out of town, Sophie?"

"It's just a matter of having enough cash, Chunky. I tol' you. Her lawyer's gonna tip her off when Stan's coming out, and then she'll scram out. But I don't know for sure, she don't tell me nothin'."

"You're still her mother, Sophie."

"Hah, that's a tired laugh. I don't even know my own daughter. When we come up here from Georgia, she was just out for a good time—fancy clothes, dancing, dates, shows every night. Now she's hard as nails. All she ever thinks about is money, money, money. She took a course in one of those charm schools and all I hear now is that she's gonna become a movie star. And she tells me straight out that she's going alone. You wouldn't think she was my own flesh and blood. It's enough to break a mother's heart."

"Uh-huh," Chunky grunted, getting up from the table.

Sophie would go on like that all night if he let her. And he had no time. He had to go upstairs to his room and really sit down and think. If Fran was going to pull out any day now, he'd have to act fast. Did Sophie think he was going to whip out a hundred-dollar bill to dry her tears with? Hah! But for Fran—that was another story. It might just pay to keep a spare hundred in the room. Just in case. It would be worth a hundred to have her for even just once.

Slowly he walked up the rickety stairs. There was a light on in Fran's room and the door was half open. When he got to the landing he kicked off his shoes and tiptoed along the wall opposite from Fran's door.

She was lying on the bed reading a magazine. Her skin was smooth and perfumed. Nothing in Chunky's dirty existence was as clean as that woman. He wanted to be near that cleanness.

All she was wearing were a bra and panties. He held his breath and let his eyes travel down. Fran rustled a page of her magazine, glanced at it for a second, and let it drop to her side. As she reached up to put out the bedlight, she tugged at the teasing bits of cloth and kicked them off entirely. Her whole body moved in this action, breasts jiggling, legs twisting closed, and then she gave one long glance down the length of her nude body and turned out the light.

Chunky's face was flushed with a deep crimson. His breath came spasmodically, chokingly. He inched again down the hall to his own room, vowing that the next bed she would do that little act on would be his own. And soon.

If she only knew, he grinned. If she only knew how much of a show she gave away for free. She'd never forgive herself. For a miser like Chunky, this was as good as getting sixth row center to the biggest hit on Broadway.

In the dark, Fran waited to hear the footsteps fade away, listened for the key in Chunky's door.

I hope, she thought, that old dog saw enough to make him hungry for the main course. Christi I could feel his hot little eyes boring into me like drills. For a second there, when I heard his breath come so heavy, I thought he'd flip and come barging in here.

Jeezus, she thought. What if the old geezer wasn't able to do anything with her? And her showing herself off like that—for nothing. Well, she'd find out about that soon enough. No man would make a pass unless he knew he could carry through. The thing was to see if he'd reach for her. They would have to be alone for that.

Lord, what she had to do for money! Showing herself off like that in front of a wheezing old man.

Now, in front of a young bull like Leroy—that would be fun. Real fun. But Leroy didn't have a lot of money hidden away like old Chunky. And Leroy could hurt her like that bastard of a husband of hers, Stan. No man would use her like five pounds of wet liver again. No man. She'd see to that; it would be her way or not at all.

When she fell asleep she dreamed that Leroy stood before her, naked, eager, ready for her. He was plastered all over with hundred-dollar bills. She came toward him to peel off the money. As each bill came off, the skin underneath became the old, gray flesh of Chunky. Fran peeled faster and faster, and more and more of Leroy turned into Chunky. When she came to his loins, she stopped peeling, but the figure, half Leroy, half Chunky, came toward her. As it stood directly over her, peering down on her as she was backed against the wall, she became overcome with desire and she reached out to take off the last bill covering the man. Just then it burst into flame.

When Fran woke up in the morning, her pillow was covered with tears, and she felt that she had ridden sleeplessly through hell and back again.

CHAPTER THREE

LEROY got off the bus at the downtown *Walgreen's* a few minutes early. Fran had asked him to window-shop for himself. She wanted him to look at a new model phonograph that she told him he could get for fifteen percent less through her. Fran had brought the subject of music so often into their conversations these past few weeks that Leroy felt almost honor bound to buy a phonograph. Fran mentioned how she liked to relax around the house while a stack of phonograph records spun on.

Now he wanted one of his own. It just might serve as the right inducement for Fran to come to his own one-room apartment.

While he scanned the brightly lit windows, he thought about what Fran and he planned for tonight. It would be another evening of house hunting. Though he was shelling out almost a whole day's pay already for various items he bought from Fran on the installment plan, she still badgered him into looking for a house.

For Edna, she used to say as she dragged him on the buses two or three evenings a week. And, because he wanted to be with her more than anything else in his life, he tagged along after her. Sometimes he went without a decent lunch or supper in order to meet those time payments, but still, after she appealed to his conscience as a husband, he went out again looking for a house.

Where the money for it would come from, he didn't really know. In a way, as Leroy figured it, he was paying out so much to Fran now in time payments that he could be actually keeping her for just about the same cost.

And all she had given him so far was companionship. Whenever he'd try to walk with her through the park or back streets, she'd start mentioning Edna, and how Edna must be missing him. She had a way of making him appear to be a real virile character, and still she personally didn't give him a tumble. But, oh, how she could go on with talk about how Edna was the luckiest woman alive to have such a guy to call her man.

It was so goddam teasing. Then Fran would smile at him kind of low-lashed, and he would forget her taunting ways, her dragging in of Edna, and just think about her as his girl, his alone.

He was standing by the bus stop, waiting for her to come by, full of thoughts about where they would go after the evening's house hunting, when his thoughts were seemingly answered by the conversation of two fellows loitering nearby. He recognized them as close pals of Sailor Sedlak.

As if coming in on cue, the shorter one, a thick-set, surprisingly thin-faced guy was saying, "No, Steve, I don't figure *The Red Barn* at all. That's a name that's too damn accurate for my blood. Whole place is infested with hillbillies. Looks like a dance hall out of *Tobacco Road*."

"Yeah, Phil, I know," his friend a blond stick of a man, confirmed. "They got a jukebox there now that plays nothing but Grand Old Opry records. And they bring their women there, too. Smells like a hayloft whorehouse."

"Well, the jail smells like a hayloft, too. A hayloft soaked in alcohol. Mike, the cop on this beat, tells me that so many of them are hauled in on a Saturday night for drunkenness that they plan to charge admission to keep out the riffraff."

"Boy, if that weren't so goddam true it would be funny."

A third man came out of the movie, on the corner, and walked toward them. The three of them soon swaggered up the block together. When they strutted past Leroy, they let out a jangle of farm noises right in his face.

He was just about to lam into them when, from the corner of his eye, he noted a shimmering vision in golden yellow coming off the bus.

"Fran, Fran, where you been? I've been here waiting and itching for a good fight with those bastards parading away there. What a lousy town it is when two guys who are workers in the same shop hate me 'cause I come from the hills and they don't."

She stood in front of him, not speaking, but raising her long hair up onto her head and fixing it there with a few tiny pins. Her milk-white neck and curve of shoulder came into view. Across her pert face, bright with small, sharp features, came a tantalizing grin.

"This'll probably make you hotter, putting my hair up, but it makes me cooler. And stop talking about guys hating you. You're such a nice lug nobody—but nobody—could hate you."

"Sorry to bother you with my griping, Fran," Leroy apologized. "Where do we get that bus for the house you want me to see?"

"Across the street. And, oh Leroy, maybe you could think a little about buying a nice secondhand car? In the winter the bus transportation isn't reliable, and—"

"Lord, Fran, I'll hardly eat at all after paying the fancy rent on one of these houses. Where'n hell am I going to get the kind of money I'd need for a car?"

"Well, you could take out a long-term loan. They don't cost much, and you don't have to start paying for months and months. Honest, Leroy."

"Forget it, Fran. Let's look at that house."

They went across the street and took another bus that sloped downhill as it traveled along. Alongside him, Fran sat silently, pretending to be hurt by his refusal to consider a loan. Actually, she was thinking fiercely about how to coax him into it. Maybe she had pushed him too far. Maybe the bait was getting stale.

They'd go out tonight, go out big. And then she'd let him convince her to come to his apartment. Oh, she wouldn't go all the way, just enough to make him set his heart on a lot more of the same. He ought to be real starved for a little loving by this time. It ought to be a crazy kind of an evening, Fran thought. In her mind she began to plan the various turns of conversation that would get him into the state she wanted him in.

But first—how to get him to rent a house. That was the thing. Charley Bruxton, the guy who owned the shack they were going to see tonight, promised her thirty percent commission if Leroy rented it. For thirty percent she'd torture him into it!

Leroy watched the houses as the bus sped by. What would the house tonight look like? For weeks Fran had dragged him around to see clapboard houses that looked like glorified Rock Slide outhouses. And the prices they charged, only a movie star could pay. Yet Fran told him that this was the going price. Thank the Lord for her, Leroy said to himself. Without Fran he knew that he would be taken for everything he had. Which wasn't much, that was for sure.

He'd like something a little better at least than what he was born and raised in back home. There, a house meant a pile of boards nailed up in the shape of a box. The roof leaked, heat blazed in the summer, the walls froze over in the winter. It didn't bother Edna none, but for Leroy it was living just like the animals, only the animals were living better because the farmers took better care of them than of their own families.

The bus lurched and his knee struck hers. She turned to look at him.

"You're still angry with me, Fran?" Leroy asked shyly.

"No, fella, I'm just sort of quietly looking you over. My gosh, in that new outfit you look like a new man. And it didn't cost much, did it? Truth, now?"

He had to admit that he looked like a magazine ad. He wore light gray slacks and a wine-colored sport shirt made out of some lightweight material. Fran helped pick it out and personally went and argued the salesman into a decent price.

"I'm managing, kid. Managing, and that's about all."

"Well, Edna'll sure be impressed. By the way, Leroy, have you heard from Edna? She must be waiting for the good news that you've got a house."

"Edna and I don't write much," Leroy replied, wishing that Fran would mention Edna in a tone of jealous anger. She remained so damn unconcerned.

"Here it is, Leroy. Our stop. Let's get off and get to it. And I hope you won't be so damn fussy."

They got off the bus, and together, arm in arm, they stood on the sidewalk. Leroy surveyed the area as though he was the first settler to come there. He liked the fairly open spaces he saw around him. The houses weren't so shacklike as he'd been seeing, and on some of the lots little gardens had been started. Each house had a patch of land for itself the size of a small dance floor.

"Gee, Fran, I could build myself a little garden here. I really could."

"Now that's the first bright thing you've said since we started looking for a place. I know how important it is for you to plant something and watch it grow. My gosh, it's your whole life."

Fran's calculated remark had its desired effect.

"You're really an understanding woman, Fran," Leroy said warmly. He put his arm around her and drew her to him. For a few seconds she permitted his arm to encircle her. Then she drew away, not abruptly, but slowly, as though it were a real effort for her to tear herself away. It's like baiting the trap with a little honey instead of cheese, she smiled to herself.

She led him down the street and turned right at the corner. Here, the homes were running to seed. They stopped at a shabby brown house. The paint peeled off from splitting clapboards. The low front porch had started to sag. A house number was chalked on the door.

Fran was leading Leroy up the rutted walk when, from the next house, a dilapidated building in a similar state of decay, a young Negro boy came prancing out. He dashed back in again for a second and came out with a broom. Slowly, with a little dance to his steps, he began to sweep the porch.

Leroy looked at Fran, and she knew without speaking that she would never in all the world convince Leroy to rent this house.

"You never know, do you?" She shook her head in seeming disbelief of the sight of the industriously sweeping Negro boy.

They went on walking.

Four or five blocks farther they found a little neighborhood tavern that was nearly empty. A fat, balding proprietor turned up the electric fan when he saw them enter. They ordered beer after beer and spent more than an hour holding hands in the shadowed corner, out of sight of the blaring television set.

"There'll be another lead real soon, Leroy. I'll have a lead for you before the week is over. You'll see."

The disappointment had made Leroy kind of blue. Here he was alone in a strange city, fighting hard not to fall in love with a married woman (he being married himself), and all the time wanting her something fierce. It was all getting a little too much for him. He wanted to see the familiar outlines of his land, he wanted the old faces surrounding him. He wanted to be home.

"I've been thinking, Fran. I'd sure like to get back home, see the farm and the folks. Think it could be managed?"

"They need help really bad, Leroy, so I think they'll overlook a leave for a couple of days. But why don't you wait until you get a house. Then just bring Edna back with you and settle down."

"No, I'm worried about Edna. She don't write or nothing. Maybe she don't figure on coming back with me at all."

He stared at Fran intently, hoping to see some reaction in her face. He wasn't sure himself whether or not he wanted Edna back. A little encouragement from Fran and he wouldn't be so confused.

"For a guy like you, any girl would *fly* home," Fran said as she leaned across the table. Perfume from the cleavage in her breasts overcame the beer stench. Leroy's eyes became half-lidded. Absent-mindedly, she stroked his bare forearm with her fingers, curling the hairs along it.

"Well, I decided that Edna deserves a taste of city life same as me," Leroy said, running his hand across the faintly moist wrist Fran extended to him. "We'll rent a house for the winter, and then, come spring, we'll look around for that farm I've been wanting. Doesn't seem to be anything to keep me here in town once I've saved a little money."

At last his hinting struck home.

"You got me now, Leroy. Come on, let's get out of here. I crave some excitement. What about the stock-car races?"

"Sure."

A night out on the town had become the accepted procedure after house hunting. Sometimes it was a movie, a night club, the races, wrestling matches. Nothing really excited him except seeing the thrill on Fran's face as she got caught up in the lights and the movement and the noise of the entertainment. When she was delighted, she would press her arm against his. Once she kissed him impulsively and passionately.

"And listen, if we see Sailor there, Leroy, stay away from him. He's a mean one and I know he's out to get you."

"I can take care of myself."

"Well, you just watch your step."

Her eyes crinkled then widened in admiration of him. She seemed to appraise him, estimate his strength and fighting ability.

"Would you care if I fought, Fran?"

"I like a winner, Leroy—and I think you're a champ."

The track that night seemed electric with excitement. Leroy felt charged through with an energy he had almost forgotten he had. But Fran was soon bored, and coaxed him into leaving. They made their way through the crowds. Leroy looked for a bus stop.

"We're not taking a bus, are we, Leroy?"

"It's only a short ride to *Eddie's*. That's where you want to go for drinks, isn't it, Fran?"

"Look," she said, taking a stance like a posturing fighter, legs planted solidly and wide apart, "if we can't go in a car—that you don't have, by the way—let's go in a cab, like decent people."

She turned to walk away, but Leroy caught her by the shoulder and held hard.

"You're hurting me, Leroy."

"Okay, we'll take that cab, but understand this—"

Then she did a strange thing. Fran turned her face, twisted it so that her cheek brushed gently across Leroy's hand as it gripped her shoulder.

"You're a real strong boy," she murmured. "I like you real fine, but you *are* hurting me."

Gentled by her soft way sprung on him so suddenly, Leroy released her and called the cab that stopped near them to wait out the light.

As soon as they settled down, Fran snuggled up close to him. The cab lurched around a corner and her hair brushed across Leroy's face. He grasped some of it in his fingers and kissed it with a burst of small, quick kisses.

"My, aren't we passionate," Fran said, suddenly aware she was responding to him. She felt his grip and a quick warmth ran through her.

"You do like me, at least a little, don't you, Fran?"

"Sure, sure, Leroy."

She let her lips caress his neck and became aware of the pulse throbbing behind his ear. With the edge of her moist tongue she cooled it.

Suddenly Leroy buried his face against her blouse. His arms clasped her as though she were his very salvation.

She patted his head in mild rebuke; her voice became thoughtful and controlled again.

"You're a great guy, Leroy. But I'm not a hillbilly floozie that you can get with a can of beer and a bowl of potato chips. I like a good time, and that costs money. Just remember that and we'll get along fine, even better than we do now."

In a way, though he had never slept with her, Leroy felt more of a man being with her than after all his years of being Edna's husband. When he was with Fran he became aware of the power in his muscles, of the effect of his smile on her mood, of the way she looked at him when she noticed desire becoming apparent through his thickened voice and lowered eyes.

Everything about her, even the innocence of her clean, soap smell excited him. And even the slightest indifference toward him was enough to ruin a night's sleep.

In his saner moments Leroy realized that she was luring him on with a fervent good-night kiss and nothing more. It was a bribe, he knew during this lucid period, but the bribe became a dope, something he had to have week after week. But like a dope, the kiss soon lost its effect. Leroy yearned for something more, as the marijuana addict soon yearns for heroin, and sitting there in the cab, watching her eyes sparkle with vivacity, Leroy knew he wanted her as a complete woman, not just a pair of lips that taunted and frustrated him.

The neighborhood crowd, the last-bottle-of-beer-before-bed crowd, was just leaving *Eddie's* when Fran and Leroy entered. The air conditioning made a too-cold chill around them. A blaring jukebox mercifully drowned out the stilted dialogue coming from an ancient movie being shown on TV.

They ordered, and Fran immediately began to wave to various persons around the room. Wherever they went, Fran knew people. How did her husband stand it? Leroy wondered. And then another thought hit him: was it in her husband's company that Fran made the tour of the local clubs?

Why did she never mention her husband to him? Perhaps Sailor Sedlak was just getting his goat when he mentioned she had a husband in jail.

It could be, too, that Fran was really married, but afraid to mention it for fear she would then feel obligated to break off their relationship. So he remained silent.

"Let's dance, Leroy. Oh, excuse me—I forget you hillbillies don't dance city-style."

"Now don't start after me to take more lessons, Fran. The cost is just too damn much, what with everything else I'm paying for. I buy just about everything you say I should."

But Fran didn't urge him at all. Her attention was drawn to a young man who was slowly making his way to their table. A warm smile was fixed on his face and he was increasing it, like turning on a brighter light, as he neared Fran.

"Gee, Ray, it sure is good to see you," Fran said as she clasped his hand energetically. "Say, this is Leroy, one of the gang from the plant."

The square-set, sloping-shouldered fellow named Ray glanced quickly at Leroy and turned his attention again to Fran. Leroy was left feeling like two cents. "Just one of the gang from the plant," Fran had said so casually.

"What about a dance, Fran?" Ray said, already helping her rise from her chair.

"D'you mind, Leroy?" Fran asked coolly. She was out of her chair and snuggled in Ray's arms before she heard his answer.

Watching them dance together, Leroy couldn't remember a time when she had been so animated with him. Fran and Ray danced together as though they were long separated lovers. Leroy smarted with embarrassment. He felt that every smile in the room was directed at him, was inspired by his humiliation.

The food came. Ray pulled up a chair and joined them, and when he asked Fran to dance again, Fran didn't even make the pretense of asking Leroy's permission. He had never felt more unwanted and hurt.

He stared into his plate morosely, wondering what he had done or not done to make Fran so indifferent, when he became aware of her perfume behind him.

"Look, Leroy, Ray has a swell new Buick and he wants to take me home." Her voice was small, somewhat pleading. It was as though she were apologizing. "You know how crazy I am about these big new cars, and—well, *could* he take me home?"

Leroy sat silently.

"Hon, you know you haven't been exactly enjoying yourself. And Ray and me have a lot to talk about. So why don't you get home and get a night's sleep."

"I'll get a bus. Go 'head, dance with him."

She pretended not to notice the great effort with which he controlled himself.

"Sure, get a bus. It's only a quarter. Even a cheapie like you won't complain about that."

Leroy stole out of *Eddie's* as though he had done a shameful thing. He couldn't hold his head up, and his hands were jammed into his pockets to prevent him from striking out at the first person or thing he came into contact with.

How could she do this to him, he wondered, not even being able to really curse her out. Disillusionment, like a searing pain, swept through his body.

Like a final nail in his personal crucifixion, Leroy stood suffering as he heard a group of people lash out against the migrant workers. A gang of young factory hands out for a night on the town had paused in front of *Eddie's,* blocking Leroy's exit to the street.

"They don't even bother to wear coats," a thin, ratfaced machinist said. "You'd think that they weren't bright enough to know what to do with the buttons?"

Leroy remembered that he too had not worn a coat. Ashamed, he was about to move away, but the fellows regrouped about another speaker, a narrow-shouldered youth with a wizened face.

"… and we're stuck with 'em, the whole goddam lot of them. The town is ruined."

"Boy, that's the truth," a third chimed in. His voice gathered a ferocious momentum of hate as he went on. "The town just lives off of 'em like a pack of bloodsuckers. They sell 'em TV sets, used cars, fancy clothes and New York type furniture. The rest of us family people are supposed to sit by and see them live better than us."

The last speaker suddenly stopped talking, as though he were exasperated and defeated by the terrible situation.

"C'mon," he said, urging his comrades into motion. "Let's get moving, I'll be damned if I'm gonna sit and eat with them in a public restaurant. Bad enough I've got to eat with them in the plant cafeteria."

The rage Leroy had been suffering began to spill out. He pushed himself in front of the fellow who seemed the leader.

"All right, you crummy bastard. You've said enough. Let's fight. Let's fight it out now."

He was about to take a well-powered swing, when a restraining hand caught his wrist. He swerved around, ready to battle this enemy first, when he noticed instantly that it was an old friend from a town near Rock Slide.

"Marty Packer!" Leroy cried excitedly. "How the hell are you? Boy, you come up at me like the avenging angel. Why haven't I seen you before. When—"

"Hey, hold on. Let's get away from these bully-boys."

With startling suddenness, a mood of reunion, of joviality, swept over Leroy, and almost regally he and Marty extended

their hands in front of them and made space between the hostile group. The toughs parted from them a little awed and shaky. They weren't ready for a fight, because if they knew anything about these Ozark hicks, they knew that they were powerful hulks of men.

Leroy and Marty walked down the corner to the little public square, a few rusting benches and a tired, hangdog tree.

"I just haven't had a chance to get to you, Leroy. I been so busy putting in overtime. Some weeks I put in twenty hours of overtime."

"Hell, what are you knocking yourself out for?"

"Boy, it ain't for me. Let me tell you that straight off. I am, as the saying goes, feeding a loan shark my blood. My blood, my sweat, and a few tears, too. I took out a loan and the interest piles up higher and quicker than a floodtide back home."

"What did you buy, Marty—a fleet of Cadillacs?"

"I just bought what a pretty young miss told me was the basic essentials in life—an old secondhand car, a radio, a TV, a washing machine for my wife Sara Jane, and a couple of decent suits."

"Boy, I bet some super-salesman got a hold of you."

"Nope, just a blonde little trick with the tightest, cutest little behind I ever had the pleasure of—uh—seeing."

"What she do? Own a department store?"

"No, but she seemed to know someone who did. Man, she sold me everything but my own nuts."

"And you let yourself buy it. Listen, Marty—"

But Leroy didn't go on. The girl Marty described was a blonde. Fran was a real enough looking redhead. And yet their ways could have made them both sisters; they worked so much alike. Or did they? Leroy realized that he was furiously hurt and bitter because of Fran's cruel indifference. He would accuse her of almost anything in his anger—even of trying to fleece him.

"What were you saying, Leroy?" Marty looked dolefully ahead as though he was making his debt calculations in his mind.

"Nothing. I can't say anything, Marty, 'cause I've been buying like crazy, too."

"Well, don't let the loan sharks get you."

"No. Listen, don't get mad but I've had a rough night. Do you mind if I hop this bus and get on home? I feel low enough to throw myself under it, but I'll change my mind and jump on board."

"Sure, Leroy. 'Money is the root of all evil and the flowering tree of all melancholy.' That was a saying of my Uncle Sugar Jack."

"Your Uncle Sugar Jack was a wise man."

"Wise enough to pay cash for everything."

The bus came and parked right in front of the little public square. In his mind Leroy could still hear Fran's happy scream of abandoned laughter rise above the jukebox, and the answering guffaw of Ray's booming voice.

The pickup of the bus cut into Leroy's thoughts as he entered, but nothing, not even the weight of the fat woman who pushed against him and stood on his foot, could crush his misery out of existence.

CHAPTER FOUR

THE sounds and sights and smells of morning attacked Fran like so many warriors the next morning. In a state of being *almost* awake, she became aware of the familiar heavy tread of Sophie on the stairway outside her door, of the orangey presence of the sun against her eyelids as it battled through the unwashed window, and of the odor of fresh coffee (it would have to last all day, Fran knew) and frying eggs. This assault upon her senses defeated her too early in the day; she was a victim of a riotous evening before.

Ray had been fun. For a second or so her conscience had bothered her about her callous treatment of Leroy, but then, close against the familiar side of Ray as she nestled against him in his car, the delight of being made love to overcame her doubts.

Fran could let herself go with a man like Ray. She had no commitments to him. They caressed, they kissed, they enveloped themselves with each other—and only minutes later they were as far apart as strangers. No responsibilities, not for either of them. There was no burden of unreturned affection lurking in her heart after being with Ray as there was with Leroy.

The trouble with Leroy was that he was too damn decent; he was more than something in pants. He was a human being, and because of it, because of the binding need he showed for her, Fran reacted defensively, by teasing and bitching and going hot and cold with him. Send up a smoke screen was her motto. Don't let the guy get too close or he'll get to know that you too can form attachments and get hurt. Fran vowed after Stan went into stir that she would never let any man hurt her physically or emotionally again.

In a few moments Sophie would come banging on the door, urging her to get up and get dressed. Fran took advantage of her privacy by gathering her thoughts together, thoughts of how her savings were coming, of what she would do when her new life began; thoughts, too, of Stan.

From the next room, through the cardboard-thin walls so sloppily whitewashed, came the laughing murmurs and sounds of a couple making love.

Stan used to like to make love in the early hours of the morning. Often she would awaken a few moments before him and watch him as he rose from his dark world of sleep into the world of light. He would stretch his long frame; then lazily, his motions displaying the sureness he felt, he would turn, still with eyes closed, and find the warmth of her, explore her with delicate, then possessive probings. She remembered those mornings in each vivid detail, and remembered, also, that for hours afterwards she would wear over her flesh, like some irresistibly arousing invisible garment, the touch and feel and warmth of him.

She had not been made love to like that for over a year now. Ray had had her as he would a faceless, formless mass of female flesh. She knew that he was indifferent, even bored with her. What she wanted again was the searching, driving involvement of a man who cared at least a little. For Fran it didn't have to be a lot of affection, but at least a little.

She realized now it was not affection she had got from Stan. Except for his body, he had none, and she hated him for the cruelty he showed to her, despised him even more because she could not forget the thrills he burned in her when he was filled only with desire and not sadism.

If she wanted loving now, Fran knew, it would have to be from Leroy. Well, she could handle him if he got too sticky with his sentimental attachments. She could always play on his conscience, his cheating on Edna, reminding him of it if he dared to suggest something more permanent with her.

But he was such a poor soul. Maybe all right for a while, but she wanted money, Fran did. And she would get it. And only one guy she knew had the money—old Chunky. And she knew he'd give some of it over to her, maybe one hundred bucks at a time, if she gave herself to him.

Well, Stan would be out soon. She needed to get to California, and a few extra hundred would come in handy. No matter how she got it.

But first, to get Chunky to know she was available. The Big Pitch—getting him to reveal where he stored his cache of money—would have to wait. After she got that, there'd be no more waiting for her. She'd be off to California in a superjet.

She was startled out of her reverie by the voice of Sophie nagging her to get downstairs. While she dressed the thought of Leroy, and how she was going to get him to plunk some money down on a house, and then a car, and then—Well, first things first, decided Fran, as she slipped into a pair of almost transparent panties. Over these, and a skimpy bra, she wrapped a kimono of sultry red-orange velvet leaves on a black satin background. Behind her ears and in the cleavage of her breasts she sprayed a heavy-scented perfume. Its odor was that of an intense rose.

Quite a performance for a mere breakfast with the family, Fran thought sardonically. But in a moment she knew her efforts were not in vain, for from below she heard Chunky's wheezy voice.

Quickly, in stockinged feet, she went down the stairs to the parlor door. It was open about two inches. Inside she noticed that three men were talking in a huddle around Chunky. Finally, one of them threw up his hands in disgust, slapped them resignedly against his sides and fished into his pockets. He extracted a wad of bills and jammed them into Chunky's already outstretched palm.

Where does that money go into? Fran wondered. What does a whole great pile of it look like? What does an old geezer like that *need* with all that dough?

But all Chunky did with the money was to crumple it and push it into the right-hand pocket of his greasy, unpressed khaki pants. Then, as if remembering, he reached in and took out a single bill and smoothed it between his fingers.

Strange, Fran, mused, very strange. What was he up to?

The trio of thieves glanced around the room and suddenly walked out the door leading to the auto graveyard. No goodbyes, no small talk. Chunky was alone.

"You can come in now, Fran," he said, a tone of smugness in his old-man's voice. "You'll catch cold out there in the drafty hall."

"Why, you sneaky letch! You—how did you see me?"

"I saw your reflection in that hood's eyeglasses."

"Boy, you got some eyesight, grampa."

"Details, too. I saw that hungry look come into your eye when you saw me take out that C-note."

"A C-note. Who you trying to impress?"

"You, you dumb broad. Who else?"

The surprise of being discovered had disconcerted Fran's bearing. She slumped, and the top and bottom of the kimono pushed forward. Her rounded, fully curved breasts jerked suddenly as if in alarm. Her smooth thighs showed from the silky folds of the kimono.

Chunky looked at her and salivated slightly. She saw his eyes widen and his teeth pull at his lip. Red crept up into his neck.

Fran stood motionless. Why, that tired old goat wants me as hot and heavy as a young buck, she realized in utter amazement. The nerve of him. Waving that hundred-dollar bill in front of her like she was a trained dog, ready to leap up and bite and beg for it. Screw him! Not even for a thousand would she lay for him.

Then Fran remembered her pocketbook lying in her bureau drawer. In its secret compartment was her bank book. Old Chunky could make a nice, impressive contribution to that little book. It would make some very interesting reading. And it would mean an end to the endless conniving and fleecing rubes, then conning them into the teeth of the loan sharks. She could start being a real lady sooner than she had even planned. What finally decided it for Fran was her inborn knowledge as a woman that she could give her body to a man without giving anything of herself. More than that, she could even keep him from enjoying it.

Yes, she finally admitted to herself, Chunky might have her—but she'd leave a wound in his mind that would take any pleasure out of his memory forever.

She went slowly toward him. With one hand she planned to reach for the hundred-dollar bill; with the other she would kiss him. This would tell him that she would be his woman for a night.

As she reached within range of his grimy stench and aged, unkempt appearance, her mother pushed her bulk into the parlor.

"I heard you come down, Fran, but I didn't know you was here. C'mon in for breakfast."

"Coming, Ma. Just coming now." She reached for Chunky's hand, now closed like a fist, and tried to pry it open to get at the bill. "I'll be going right up to take a nice, slow, hot tub as soon as breakfast's over, though."

She said it directly to Chunky. He grinned; he leered.

"Well, you'll have the place to yourself. Renie and me is going to the beach, and the rooms are all empty already."

"Good, I like my privacy. You can't pay too much for privacy, I always say."

"That's right, Fran," Chunky said. "Whatever your privacy costs, it must be a bargain, though."

The three went in for a real family breakfast together.

Chunky couldn't take his eyes from Fran all during the meal. Each time she stretched or yawned or leaned forward over the cluttered table, he would stop shoveling food into his half-tooth-less mouth, and glare at her hungrily, impatiently.

"You know," Sophie was saying as she cleared the dishes, "I guess Renie and me'll go see the new Clark Gable movie. It's a helluva lot cooler in a movie than on the beach. And that Gable—he's my man! Whyn't you come, Fran?"

"No, Ma, I'll stay here. Anyway, I like my men in the flesh, if you know what I mean."

Chunky nudged his foot against Fran's under the table. Fran hesitated for a moment and then nudged back. What the hell, she thought, play around with this old tomcat once, twice, then find out where he keeps that treasure, and you'll never again have to be with any man you didn't really want.

"I'd sure like to ask a favor of you, Chunky," Sophie said, attempting to twist her face into a pretty smile. "Would you mind driving Renie and me to the movie. It's so hot, and the buses just crawl."

For a second Fran became furious. She wanted Chunky alone in the house with her; he had to be baited as soon as possible. But then another idea flashed through her mind, really the best solution to her problem.

"Sure, Chunky, run along," Fran said. "Then you can come back and maybe we'll play a little Michigan Rummy together. You'd like that, wouldn't you, if we played ... cards together?"

"All right, Sophie. I'll drive you. You take a hot bath, Fran, and be ready for a little game when I come back. Okay?"

Fran nodded. How could Sophie be so stupid, she thought. Or was she crazy like a fox? Did Sophie know that Fran had decided to get Chunky's money even if she had to get Chunky, too?

After Sophie and Chunky had smoked a morning cigarette together, Renie came down, still disheveled and slightly hung over from last night.

"You think you can keep your eyes open for a movie?" Sophie asked as she hoisted her flabby bulk out of the chair.

Renie nodded yes, and Chunky went out to start the car.

Fran knew she didn't have much time.

"Better get to that car, girls, before he changes his mind."

Renie and Sophie waddled out after Chunky.

Fran savored the fact that she was entirely alone for an instant and then dashed up to her room.

It works in movies, Fran muttered half out loud as she poked in her bureau drawer for a penknife and a bobby pin. Finally she found them and went down the hall to Chunky's room. The quietness of the house frightened her for a moment. Each creak and scurrying of an unseen mouse seemed as witnesses to her actions.

Chunky's room was the only room that was padlocked. And for good reason, too, Fran was sure. Quietly, quickly, she worked the padlock with the penknife and bobby pin. The lock clicked. She let herself in and made straight for the dresser. On it was an old comb, a dirty hairbrush and a pawn ticket. Nothing else.

She ransacked the drawers, not furiously, but methodically, carefully rearranging everything back into its former position. The mattress was poked and searched, all his clothes, the radiator. Not a single dollar bill. Where was it? And if it weren't here, why was his room padlocked?

Then she bumped against a hatbox lying on the floor. It made an odd gurgling sound. Fran bent down and untied the string around it. Inside were more than a dozen bottles of pills, vials of liquid, and a long hyper-dermic syringe and needle. The labels on each of the bottles said the same thing, more or less—hormones, testosterone pills, virility compounds.

Revulsion swept through her. She was going to let herself be had by a man who was desperately afraid he wasn't potent. It was like being sucked into a stinking swamp. She didn't want to be part of it. She deserved fine, strong men with passion and power in their bodies, not flabby, frightened old men.

This was why he padlocked the door, to keep his secret from the world. It meant as much to him as money, his pride in his manhood. Well, now she had him! Maybe not enough to blackmail, but enough so that if he did come near her he'd never be able to take her. She would prey upon his weakness and his doubts as though she were a vulture hovering over the corpse of his virility. Each time he'd come to her, paw her, pant over her, but then she would jeer him, hurt him, and he would ultimately fail. But he would keep coming back, keep on with the money, hoping each time that he would succeed. Over her dead body, maybe; it was a grim joke, but Fran didn't even smile.

She left his room and went into the shower a few doors down. Under the hot water, surrounded by the scent of her perfumed soap, she restored a little of her self-respect. Like Narcissus gazing at his reflection in the lily pool, Fran adored her image in the bathroom mirror. With a huge powder puff she patted lilac-scented dust over her tingling skin.

She heard the old familiar rattle of Chunky's ancient Chevrolet pull into the driveway. She put on a pair of long black silk stockings, so filmy that the rosy flesh of her thighs glowed through them, attached them to a pair of delicate lace panties, and left the bathroom.

As she settled herself on the bed, after making sure that her door was an inch or two open, she heard Chunky's heavy tread on the battered staircase. His steps ceased outside the door.

"Now don't stand out in the hall and catch a draft, Chunky. Remember—that's what you told me?"

He walked in, utterly amazed at the sight of Fran in a state of semi-undress. The shades were drawn and a soft sun filtered into the room. The room was enveloped in cool shadows. Perfume choked the air. She lay with her bra strap off one shoulder. Her panties were stretched taut against her smooth, pink-skinned stomach.

Chunky, his muscles all alive now, moved toward her, a little unsteadily. The sensualism with which she had surrounded herself fired the room with a peculiarly exciting heat. As in a dream, Chunky threw off his shirt and trousers. He stood before her, an old, maddeningly enraged man, fevered with desire. When he came close enough to bend over her, she turned her head away, as though protecting herself from a blow.

"The money, Chunky. Where's the hundred?"

"Later, later," the old man said between clenched teeth. His breath came hoarsely.

"Give it to me now—just in case."

He shuffled back to his trousers and got out the bill. She took it and slammed it into her night-table drawer.

"All right, if you can, get it over with."

"I want you, Fran. I want you very much."

"Get it over with, or can't you?"

"What do you mean? What crazy talk is that? Don't you see how much I want you?"

"Wanting and doing—there's a big difference."

He got into bed beside her. His body reeked of sweat, of dirt, of the undefinable decay of old age. He began to search her body with his hands.

"Did you take all your pretty little pills, old Chunky?"

He reacted as if he had been whipped. His hands left her body as though her flesh had burned him. Bolt upright in bed, his body tense, he stared ahead.

"I was just asking—"

"How did you know, you miserable devil-bitch?"

"I know these things. A woman knows."

"What do you know?" He looked at her with fearful respect, afraid of the intuitive knowledge of her sex.

"Look at you! Your face is burning, but your body...Look, see for yourself that you're not able to have me. It's nothing, you just should have taken those pills, or the needle. Maybe the needle."

"Give me time, Fran. I'm not—"

"I know, not a young man. That, you don't have to explain. I can see for myself."

Chunky's teeth came together. In every part of his straining body he felt the perspiration cover him, a cold layer of despair. Desperately, as though Fran were going to disappear before him, he moved to her. The throbbing of her pulsing skin hit against his tired flesh like wavelets of electricity. But the current did not connect in him.

She lay cold, unmoving, rigid, feeling herself the bride of a persistent monster. Her eyes were closed, her arms drawn down close along her sides. The fingers of both hands twisted inward, the nails ripping the soft flesh of her palms. In her heart she felt a stillness, and her ears were filled with his panting, and heavy lament, the cry of frustrated incompletion.

In the half-darkness of the late afternoon she felt the shadows move over her like the presence of death. Like shovelfuls of earth above her grave, she was aware of urgings.

"Forget it, Chunky. Try again some other time. Some time when you're prepared. Take more pills—more and more!"

She spoke the words like a curse, and stricken, he moved away and lay in abject silence at her side. He could not look at her. Anger fumed within him. Words churned in floodtide turbulence in his mind. Only a single phrase was he able to utter, and that one was directed at himself.

"Please, Fran, let me try again. Let me try again soon."

"Another hundred, another chance. Buy enough and you're bound to get the door prize—some day."

She was glad she had taken the hundred earlier. There was no chance of his reneging, now.

"Here's your pants, Chunky. You'd better go."

He put them on slowly. Why wasn't he angry, Fran wondered. He should be bitching about having to spend a hundred bucks at all, especially mad now that he didn't take his pleasure.

But all he said was, "You shouldn't have gone into the room, Fran. And most of all, you shouldn't have told me what you did. That was the worst thing you ever did."

When he walked out, his head was bent low. Stand up, Fran wanted to shout to him. Stand up! She started to shout that phrase at him, but something in her would not let her say the words.

She lay back in bed, listening to the sound of his footsteps pace toward his room, heard his door close slowly.

A deep-seated wave of revulsion swept over her suddenly. She felt dirty all over. She took the money from her night table and twisted the bill in her right hand, as if that action could control her self-disgust. But it would not work, and presently she went into the bathroom and was sick.

Dragging herself back into bed, she began to think about her money, of Leroy, of Chunky, of her cruel, revengeful spirit, and, again, she was sick. Again and again.

The last thing she remembered before she passed out was that inside she must be hollow because all her guts were vomited up around the room. Hollow and lonely without insides.

Then the room overcame her.

CHAPTER FIVE

For days Fran had not seen Leroy, had avoided him with studious care. Ever since her hideous encounter with Chunky, she had withdrawn tensely and fearfully into herself. The outcome of her taunting had surprised her, had shaken her confidence in her perception of men. She had expected Chunky to explode in frustrated anger, was prepared to ward off his violent blows. Instead, he had capitulated meekly before her insults.

He must come back, Fran told herself as she walked the corridors at Power-Trak. If Chunky didn't come back, she would never know the secret hiding place of his treasure. Perhaps she had gone too far with her cruelty. What if he were so ashamed of himself now that he wouldn't come back to her? That mustn't happen; she would induce him to her room again.

As she passed the open door of Leroy's machine shop, a good deal of her poise and faith in herself was restored. There stood Leroy, the same as ever, long blond hair that refused to stay slicked toppling into his steady blue eyes that did not waver in front of the sparks from the machine. She realized the strength in the sweep of his broad back, could follow the ripple of his muscles as they moved under his half-sleeved shirt. This was the kind of a man for her—young, strong, competent. Soon, she promised herself, she would have him; it would remove the stain and memory of her hour with Chunky.

She would be casual, she decided, very casual. Just throw out some female lure, and see if he'd pick up the bait.

Rustling her skirt, she walked, a set smile of pert welcome on her face, to face Leroy and to begin again her teasing escapade with him.

Leroy stood at the wheel with his mind full of bitter and revengeful thoughts about Fran. During the several days he had not seen her, his mind had had a time to clear. He realized now that he was hardly able to eat properly because of the large amount of money he was paying out to Fran in installment obligations. Back at the farm he'd polish off a steak a day; now he lived on hamburger and spaghetti and perch fish. His closets were jammed with clothes that no one he knew would be impressed with. The shelves of his closet were filled with household appliances he did not take the trouble—or have the need—to operate. The dust collected on them while Fran collected for them. And all the while he went hungry!

What was it all for, Leroy thought angrily. Or rather, if he would be honest, who was it all for? For Fran, for Fran alone, Leroy knew. And Fran hadn't called or seen him in almost a week. What was he, what kind of a man was he, Leroy wondered, his self-disgust mounting feverishly within him. All for a kiss, maybe two. He wanted her more than he had ever wanted any other woman, and she gave him a kiss—nothing more—and took him for every cent he had, and a lot he didn't.

There was always home. Maybe, after the lousy taste of city life he had endured, it would be the best place of all. Edna was his woman. That was the way he'd once wanted it; he would be glad now when he saw her again. She knew him, understood and loved him in her way. Fran just used him, and not enough of him to make him want to come back to her for any more.

The last time he was with her, Fran had showed him how little he meant to her. To go off with another man when she saw how much he wanted her, needed her, relied on her, was like a vicious betrayal. His action now was almost the only thing he could still do and still call himself a man—leave off seeing Fran, break cleanly and completely.

Once free of her, he could start to save to buy that farm he knew he really wanted. Then he and Edna could start all over again. With a new farm and some money to furnish a nice house, Edna'd be a new woman. And she would be his woman!

Under his hands Leroy felt the whirring power of the machine. His eyes glared at the sparks. Around him he heard the almost mechanical drone of the workers' voices. But all his energies and emotions were concentrated on his great decision—to leave Fran and Power-Trak and the suffocating corruption of life in the city.

Thus he resolved that when Fran came to his department he would ignore her, not even glance in her direction. It occurred to him that he had not seen her for several days, and he began to wait impatiently for her appearance so he could quickly put himself to the test.

As he operated the machine he heard her voice from somewhere near the door. Undistracted, he continued with his work. Her heels, tapping on the tiled floor, sounded like a beckoning call. They stopped just behind him.

Resolutely, he turned around to face her. Her red hair burned in the flat factory light. The green of her blouse enclosed her full breasts, or rather displayed them. They quivered shyly, delicately, as though, separately, they repented for her whole self. Her smile was almost virginal in its subdued softness. And her eyes appealed to him meltingly. For a second, Leroy could not believe that she was the same woman. His goggles steamed, and she grew dim before him.

She approached him and removed the goggles. Though she had no perfume, Leroy responded to her as though she lured him with a saucy, secret scent. Words of reproach for her rushed to his lips, but her hand upon his forearm stilled them. Already, his feet began to walk with hers.

When they were out in the factory corridor she murmured, "Thank you," in his ears. The sound of her voice brought a welcome, long-lost softness in his life. He faced her, and felt as though her eyes caressed him.

"Coffee," he said. "Let's have some coffee."

Clinging to him, Fran fell into step with Leroy as they headed for the cafeteria.

Only Sailor Sedlak had noticed when they left the machine shop; but then, he had been watching them closely all along.

The minutes devoted to getting and setting up their coffee gave Leroy the necessary time to gather his thoughts. His anger had turned to melting gratefulness for her renewed attentions. All he could think of was a spectacularly fine way of repaying her for her kindness.

"You know, Fran, I've been thinkin' these past few days," Leroy blurted, anxious as a repentant sinner to please, "and I hear those new Buicks have damned good reputations. Where you think I can pick up one real cheap, a good used one, that is?"

For some seconds Fran kept her face blank. Inwardly she rejoiced at his willingness to forgive, forget and start all over again. She didn't really know how he was going to make the payments on a car; but then she really didn't give a damn about his ability to pay or not. The loan sharks could care all they wanted.

"I'll make some calls tonight—hon," she said, smiling angelically at him. "Could we go and look at some tonight?"

The "we" promised to Leroy a renewal of their former closeness—maybe promised even more. "Can't see why not tonight," he agreed quickly.

"You know, Leroy," Fran reminded him, "when you start looking for that farm, why, you'll really need a car. And that wishing for a farm—that's a solid idea. That's one of the reasons I like you so—very much, 'cause you think about the future and do something about it."

Leroy glowed like a Congressional Medal of Honor winner when he heard Fran praise him. The healing of the split between them suppressed for the moment his desire to wonder out loud about his ability to meet the new payments the car would need.

They chatted amiably for fifteen minutes. Occasionally Fran would idly play with Leroy's fingers as they tapped on the table. The coffee break over, they went their separate ways, each promising the other to meet on time that night outside the main entrance of the factory.

Shortly before three P.M., Leroy went into the washroom. Since he had left Fran that morning he'd thought of nothing else but his elation at patching things up with her, and of his self-contempt at having surrendered so easily to her. He knew now that he had to settle his relationship with Fran one way or the other. The thoughts he had of her were driving him into a frenzy of frustration. The unanswered situation with Edna tortured his conscience. Until his pursuit of Fran had ended, buying a farm was a minor matter. Starting immediately, just after they had finished looking at some cars, he would take a bold, decisively aggressive course of action.

Two other grinding machine operators ambled in to cool off. Their talk about baseball scores broke the chain of Leroy's thought. He dried his hands and neck lazily. When he was half-way toward the door, Sailor Sedlak swaggered in, his face set and stern.

Leroy watched him go to his locker and take out a bottle of whiskey. Though whiskey was expressly forbidden on company premises, Sailor flaunted the regulation openly. He dared any company cop to put him in his place; it would only mean another chance to display his savage strength.

"Go ahead, have a drink, hillbilly boy," Sailor said to Leroy, shoving the opened bottle under his nose.

Leroy stepped aside, folded his arms and waited. He sensed that this was the moment that Sedlak had decided on to settle the hate between them. The crisis he had been unafraidedly avoiding was here, and having settled up with Fran, Leroy planned to end this other messy business right here and now. The crisis mounted around him; tenseness was in every molecule of air.

"Whatsamatta, hillbilly boy, saving your strength for more important things?" Sailor guffawed an unmistakably dirty laugh.

"I got an appointment to keep, Sailor," Leroy said in a firm, level voice. "And I plan to keep it on time."

Sailor took another swallow of the whiskey and capped it. "I just want to ask you about the car I was talking to you about."

"Who me? What car?" Leroy asked, his hand on the doorknob.

"Why, you lardhead. You know what the hell car I mean—the little Chevie. When you gonna get it?"

Leroy's efforts to stay out of Sailor's way since their last encounter had convinced Sedlak that he was dealing with a pushover—a coward who couldn't even be provoked into a fight. Leroy's quiet answer seemed to confirm his judgment further. Arrogance flamed in Sailor's twisted mind. His fists tightened and loosened spasmodically, hungrily.

"What car is that again, Sailor?" Leroy asked. "Didn't you sell that heap to the tin can people yet?"

Leroy began to relish his ability to infuriate Sailor.

"Don't be a wise guy, Leroy. You wanta look at it, or don't you?"

The severe tone in his words made it clear that this was more than a question—it was a threatening ultimatum.

"Sorry, Sailor. But another person is showing me a good, new Buick tonight. Not brand new, but newer than that junker of yours."

"So that's what all that jawin' was about between you and Fran in the cafeteria this morning."

Now that Fran's name had been finally uttered, Leroy knew that he need say nothing more to goad Sailor to violence.

He poised himself to roll in either direction should Sailor throw a sneak punch.

"Sure, contribute to her old man's parole fund. And when that rotten killer is sprung, he'll come around and blow the nuts off the first hillbilly he catches looking at her."

"Fran has no mind to spring him, and you know it, Sailor."

"Says you. You sure know everything, or think you do until you've been bled snow-white by her—with all her TV sets, phonographs, fancy clothes, that kind of crap."

Sailor went to the locker, put the bottle away, and came back to face Leroy with bitterness etched in acid lines across his sullen face. His bullet head seemed shoved into his thick, short neck.

Casually, Leroy took a spring-blade knife out of his pocket, flipped out the blade and scraped idly at his square fingernails. The crowd in the washroom was ominously silent. They backed almost in chorus against the wall.

"You want to look at that Chevie with me tonight, Leroy, or do you want to argue about it outside the gate with me after work? And don't think that goddam knife scares me."

Leroy drew himself up proudly, defiantly. He flipped the knife closed and put it in his pocket. He opened the door of the washroom and said loudly, as if to invisible witnesses, "I don't need a knife, Sailor. And I ain't meeting you tonight or any night. But I do go home the same way every night and I wouldn't be hard to find if you were really aiming on looking."

"Okay, rube. That's the way you want it—that's the way it's gonna be."

Sailor jerked his head and clicked his thumb and forefinger. Like trained slaves, several of the men, his shadowlike cronies, followed Sailor out the door.

Leroy stood there, relieved at last to have the whole gritty mess out in the open. For a long time his feelings had had no outlet, and they had mounted to dangerous intensity. All his bottled-up energy waited to be translated into brutal combat with Sailor. His anger with the hillbilly-hating city folk would be released with each crashing fist. All the resentment would be buried as his knuckles stabbed brutally in the beery flabbiness of Sailor's stomach. Perhaps this slambang would be the best thing—it would give him a push onto a new track. And Fran would be there. She would see the whole thing. If he licked Sailor, Leroy knew it would count a lot with Fran. She would respond to this overt display of virility. In a way, the fight with Sedlak would be a battle to win Fran.

But would it? Again confusion rushed in on Leroy. His mind again began the old business of questioning, of doubting. He felt himself getting warm. He went again to the sinks to cool his skin. Drying himself against the coarse cloth of his work pants, he swallowed rapidly.

When the noon whistle blew he was still sitting there quietly, imagining the power of his punches, feeling them rock him to the core.

That afternoon the factory fumed with suppressed tension. Sailor spent time away from his machine like a ward-heeling politician soliciting votes. He'd go up to a man, casually flex his muscles during the simple act of reaching for a light for his cigarette. The top two buttons on his shirt remained open, conspicuously displaying the thickly matted hair on his chest. As obvious as a child showing off new clothes, Sailor impressed his overbearing masculinity upon all who would take the time to idolize him. In return, like whiskey befogging his brain, he developed a self-feeding belief in his own invincibility. Once Sailor gaily shadow-boxed in front of Leroy.

"Just a preview of coming attractions," he shouted defiantly.

At his machine, Leroy heard the grinders around him making bets on the coming fight. He was far from being the popular favorite. Suddenly he wished that Fran would not be there to see it. If he should lose, and Fran should see it, it would be the most terrible disgrace of his life. There would be the ruin of everything he had been striving for crashing around him in his defeat.

"Sailor'll belt him to hell with that left of his," one voice said as its owner bet five dollars against Leroy.

Leroy was plain worried. He didn't have a left, or a right, for that matter. All he knew how to do was to wade in, ward off the toughest of the blows, and get his licks in whenever he caught the man in an unguarded moment. And what was it all for, anyway? He didn't like Sailor—no one did. But he had nothing special against that big windy showoff. He was *forced* to fight, forced pure and simple. Back on the farm they'd settle this by getting rip-roaring drunk together, and next morning the two of them wouldn't be able to remember what they were arguing about in the first place. The city, though, demanded sterner justice. And Leroy had never run away from a fight yet.

Somewhere someone dropped a wrench. It clanged and reverberated sharply. Leroy snapped awake from his daydreaming, looked at his work card, and plunged in to make up his quota for the day.

He worked with deep absorption for over two hours, and then the quitting whistle blew. A smothering silence ran through the shop. As he left his bench and walked toward the shower, Leroy was given a wide berth by the other men. They made him feel like a fighter walking slowly down the aisle at an arena. Around him some rambunctious guys struck fighting poses.

In the shower he waited for an empty stall, bathed methodically, and donned street clothing. Like a vise tightening on a sponge, his stomach seemed to grip a growing fear. A light sweat broke out all over his body.

Leroy walked in the loose-jointed gait of a hill country man. The mid-summer sun burned in a feverish effort to regather its afternoon strength. Along the gate of the factory a crowd had formed. Their voices became hushed when Leroy appeared. He saw no one, but walked across the street to the railroad siding and began to walk down the track. Carried in the wind, now stirring in the late afternoon, the jeers of the factory crew came to him. More men, he knew, would be waiting by the lot where the battle was to take place.

Piles of discarded lumber, rusty corrugated sheets of iron, neat stacks of new railroad ties, and heaps of gravel from an abandoned building project littered the vacant expanse. Informally, they grouped to form a rough inclosure; and so the lot seemed like a professional gladiators' arena.

A dozen or more of the younger machinists were standing around in small groups. When they saw Leroy, they joined together in a hard knot of hate. "Here comes that smart-ass Arkie!" someone shouted. There were a few female voices in the crowd. For them it was a treat to watch these two men bloody each other, a welcome change from boring TV shows and tame lovers.

He looks scared, Fran thought when she first caught sight of Leroy walking toward the waiting crowd. She had followed that crowd to the fight site, and at first glance she thought his walk showed hesitation. But then, looking at him, his resolute air, his determined set of jaw, she knew that he would fight hard and long, and that it would be for her. Why she felt it would be for her, she could not say; put it down to feminine intuition, she decided. But he would win, and he would win because she would be cheering him on. Her encouragement would give him the needed push he would have to have for victory.

Yes, she would cheer him on. And later they would be together and she would feel the taste of his triumph on her lips as they pressed against his. This time she would not hold back, because above all she wanted to be wanted, to be treated as a fiery, lovely woman.

Win, win, you blond, you stupid blond devil, Fran shouted to herself as she noticed Sailor come forward to meet Leroy.

Sailor hunched his heavy shoulders forward as he walked. His eyes glowed with excitement. All the muscles of his oxlike body throbbed in anticipation of battle.

"I tell you, Sailor," Leroy said as they finally faced each other at arm's length, "why you want to fight me at all, I don't know, but if it's a fight you want—"

"Lissen, hillbilly boy, if I could knock the stuffing out of just one of you haystackers, maybe the others'd take the hint and go back to feeding the pigs."

"Okay, Sailor, go ahead, make an example out of me!"

"When I get through with you, you bastard, you just better stay hidden in some outhouse in the wilds of Arkansas, 'cause your blood won't be worth water in this town if you don't."

"You sure *talk* a good fight, Sailor."

At that a fuse seemed to light in Sailor. His eyes glittered under their half-closed lids for an instant, and then he lashed out with a fast left, catching Leroy full on the mouth. Sailor bobbed his head back sharply to avoid a counterblow.

Leroy made a grasping reach for Sailor, but his arms flailed wide of the mark. Oh, if he were only back on the farm, Leroy thought for a second. He'd take a fence post or a barrel stave and whack Sailor right on the head with it.

Again Leroy lunged after Sailor, but Sailor dodged out of reach. Fancily cross-stepping, he caught Leroy with a powerfully unleashed left hand that landed high on Leroy's head, stunning him. Leroy's vision of the world flickered crazily for a moment, but soon he was again grappling his slippery antagonist.

"See, here, Leroy," Sailor razzed in a falsetto voice, "I'm bruising my tender knuckles on your hard, empty head."

"You ain't swatting mosquitoes, Leroy," some familiar voice shouted. "Keep those fists up and keep 'em closed."

"Leroy, baby, kill him, kill him for me, baby."

Fran shouted it at just the right moment. Her voice had caught Sailor by surprise, and he ducked just once the wrong way. The effect on the two men of her shrill cry was very different for each man. Leroy summoned all his wit and strength to impress Fran, to win her respect once and for all. Sailor was frightened by her. Women always did frighten him with their surprising turns from tenderness to shrieking cruelty. Men always put him at ease; men he could bully, but women were unknowable and unpredictable. He lost his nerve when he heard Fran's voice. To lose in front of her meant defeat before everyone. In a way, it would mean the collapse of his carefully constructed advertised package of himself as a man. And that he couldn't afford.

Sailor began to tire of his sport. Leroy wasn't proving enough of a real challenge. He stepped up his right-left attack, hoping to end it all in one bloody mess quickly.

Leroy licked his pulpy, battered lips and, with his one good eye, watched Sailor for a clue to his next angle of attack.

Sailor pounded at his middle with a pair of heavy blows, and Leroy's arms dropped to protect his mid-section. Set for the move, Sailor leveled a tremendous right at Leroy's head.

But his sneakers slipped in the loose ashes of an old trash fire, and his blow missed Leroy's scraped face by a fraction of an inch.

The momentum of his swing carried him toward Leroy, then beyond him as he ran three or four steps to regain his balance.

Leroy saw Sailor rushing toward him barely in time to reach for him blindly, his hands still open, and the fingers of his right hand caught the sleeve of Sailor's T-shirt and grasped it at the shoulder. The fabric began to rip, then held as Leroy leaped behind his foe and jerked at the shirt. His tugging spun Sailor around so that he faced Leroy again.

But the Sailor was off balance, and before he could throw another blow, Leroy closed on him. He threw his left arm around Sailor's waist, grasped his left wrist with his right hand, holding his left hand doubled under so the knuckles bore in at the base of Sailor's spine. Then he lunged backward, lifting the astonished Sailor off the ground.

When Sailor wriggled in mid-air, Leroy squeezed him with one fast compression of his arms and shoulders. At the peak of his effort, the muscles in Leroy's arms and shoulders stood out like gnarled oak limbs. The distended veins at his temples appeared ready to burst.

Sailor screamed once in excruciating agony as his eyes rolled backward. The short, intense expression of anguish drained the blood from the faces of the astounded spectators.

Leroy relaxed momentarily, then repeated his tremendous effort, flushing beet-red as his arms contracted, traplike, drilling his knuckles into the base of Sailor's spine. But this time there was no sound from Sailor. He hung limp in Leroy's arms, his face white as chalk.

Leroy dropped him into a shapeless heap, and stood with widespread feet as he stared down at him for a long moment. He sucked air loudly into his aching lungs and licked at his battered lips. With one shaking hand, he felt gingerly about his fast-closing right eye, the ring of spectators watching him in sullen silence.

Leroy started to move off toward the railroad tracks, then remembered his jacket. It lay near the feet of one of the shopmen, who stepped quickly aside at Leroy's approach.

Jacket in his hand, Leroy started for home again, but at the edge of the lot he paused and turned to speak to the group. "Could be his back's near busted. Better be careful when you move him."

Then he turned away. Behind him he could hear the shuffle of the shopmen's feet and their anxious murmur as they approached their vanquished champion.

"Leroy, Leroy, wait for me!"

Fran's voice was close to his ears. As he walked back to the nearest bus stop, he heard it come closer still. Then she was at his side, her arm thrust in his.

"What a guy! What a guy my man is! Did you hear me shout for you?"

He was tired, so tired that his blood seemed to have stopped in his veins, but he still heard her words, and her possessiveness awakened a part of him that had been waiting for her for a long time. Sweat ran from every pore of his body; his legs felt as weighty as dead tree stumps. But with her woman smell next to him luring him back to life, he walked with her to the bus stop. Along the way, the men congratulated him on his victory.

"I'm coming home with you, Leroy. I'm going to fix you up, *then* we'll go out to pick up a car … that is, if you still *want* to go out." She looked up at him and embraced him caressively, tenderly. "I want you," he said, murmuring it into her ears, her eyes. "I want you!"

Awash in a transport of fatigue and awakening desire, Leroy boarded the bus with Fran. He dozed a bit, and remembered only that Fran had almost lifted him out of the bus when it stopped at his home.

When he awoke she was beside him, naked and very happy and looking like she belonged in his bed with him.

CHAPTER SIX

"HELLO, champ. And a bright good morning to you."

Fran leaned over Leroy and planted a big, noisy kiss square on his lips. Sleepily he became aware of her. Her breasts were soft against his chest. Her silky hair rustled before his eyes, smothering him in a shimmering wall of perfume.

"What happened?"

"Hmm. That's just it, nothing happened. I dumped you on the bed, got your clothes off, and watched you snore away until I fell asleep myself."

"Is that true?"

"Unfortunately, that, my dear man, is *too* true."

Leroy raised himself on one elbow and grinned. This was a side of Fran he had never dreamed existed: coy, cute, a little girl full of teasing, shy humor.

He pulled the sheet off the bed and feasted his eyes on her outstretched body. The night close to him had warmed her. Through the skin on his thighs he felt her body heat, a steady touch of fevered flesh. She grew silent, and he leaned now across her and began to cover her face and ears and neck and shoulders with a steady staccato of kisses. Slowly her arms went around his neck and she drew him to her. And her eyes held his now, and then, as he came to her, their lips joined.

Afterward, they lay at each other's side in silence and in tenderness.

The tides of pleasure had not entirely ebbed from her body when Fran began to create a distance between herself and her experience with Leroy. The truth was that it had been too good. She had been able to lose herself in his vigorous love-making. And soon she would want him again, and then being with him would become a pleasant, looked-forward-to event. She would, in short, need Leroy. And that word "need" was one that Fran had banished, ever since Stan had brutally abused her.

She turned to look at Leroy, now half-dozing, watched an expression of supreme contentment flood across his relaxed face. He's feeling smug about the whole thing, the crummy bastard, Fran thought. A good lay. That's what I was. Nothing more. Well, he's right, I'm not his woman or anybody's woman. So be smug, Mr. Leroy Landers, it's one thing I won't charge you for—not outright, anyway!

For Leroy, this act of love with Fran had been the summation of all his months of hope and effort and prayer. His battered, bruised body suddenly felt charged with an excess of unchanneled energy. In a way, his fight with Sailor had toughened, exhilarated him for his intimacy with Fran. That was the way he viewed the past in these first few moments of pleasure and satisfaction. He knew now that Fran was not the bloodless, money-grubbing wench people thought she was. She was all woman. And she was his woman! He'd have to work something out now to please Edna, of course. But he'd do it. The way he felt now he could take care of three women, let alone two! Edna could get a job in the night shift; then Fran could come by, stay till dawn, then go.

His mind went lazily into a reverie in which Fran and he made love endlessly and with boundless energy. In a few moments he felt himself falling asleep. Casually, his hand reached out to gather Fran to him, to feel the warmth of her covering him as he sought his pleasure-filled rest.

"C'mon now, Leroy. Enough of that stuff. Get dressed! We got to get downtown and buy a car. Remember? Ain't you had enough? My gosh!"

Furiously, Fran disentangled herself from Leroy's grasp and leaped from the bed. She swept some clothes up in her hand and dashed into the bathroom to dress. A little stunned, Leroy began to reach for his shoes.

"No rush, Fran honey. None at all. We're gonna get a nice new Buick and then we're gonna get back here an'—"

"That's what you think, lover boy, we're gonna get the Buick all right, but as for the rest—we're then going to get a house for your wife. Remember her?"

Fran's businesslike air shocked Leroy. Her softness and sweetness disappeared in an air of self-righteous moralizing. She had no right reminding him of Edna. Not her! Not after what they had done with each other.

Seething with suppressed anger, Leroy hurried about his dressing. She gave him her love measured out like installment payments. It was a funny association for Leroy to make, and he didn't like the sound of it echoing in his mind.

Fran allowed him a few more quick kisses and then they were soon out of the house and walking toward a particular used-car lot that Fran had in mind.

"An old friend of mine, Leroy," she said, her voice smoother, almost cajoling. "He'll be glad to do a favor for me, give me a good price."

I bet he'd like to do a favor for you after all you've done for him—and for no price, Leroy thought savagely. Suddenly his suspicions of the nature of Fran's devotion to him mounted. Her businesslike affection for him provoked the hidden anxieties he had managed to repress during his months of yearning for her.

"We'll see. I'm not promising I'm buying, you know. I just say we'll see."

The used-car lot owner was a middle-aged man with slick, greasy hair that parted in the middle like a straight line down the middle of a highway. He had saggy, pouchy eyes. His skin was like the color of old cigar ashes all dried up.

"Hello, Big Joe," Fran said, clinging possessively to Leroy's arm as she almost dragged him into the lot. "Got something nice in a Buick?"

"Hello, Fran. For you, of course I got. I got the best."

Even just after it left the assembly line in Detroit, the Buick Big Joe showed Leroy would have been classified as a reject. If cars could have a personality, this car's would be schizophrenic. Attempts had been made to patch up its more obvious defects with chrome and paint. But the upholstery still sagged, the dashboard lights didn't all work, and the radio had more static than music coming out of it. The price: five hundred dollars. Two years to pay.

"My gosh, Leroy, that's only five dollars a week. Don't tell me you can't afford that. You ain't sharecropping now, you know." Fran's voice was not so much persuasive as insulting. Leroy couldn't very well refuse without appearing like a pedigree miser.

He stood there, his feet planted wide apart, appraising the car as he would a calf or a horse up for sale. The only car he had had on the farm was a 1936 Ford, and, compared to that, this '51 Buick was a bright number. But that was the way everything seemed in the city: compared to what he had at home on the farm, everything seemed fine, almost too good to be true. And yet Leroy wasn't blind; he saw the defects, the age, the uncared-for look. And still he knew he would buy it, buy it because it was still a helluva lot better than he had ever known.

Something about the air in the city, he figured, made a man itch to own fancy things. Wasn't like that on the farm, but here everyone was racing to outmatch the other guy. And with a girl like Fran you had to do more than just outmatch; you had to set world records.

"When you put it that way, that it's costing me only five a week, it doesn't seem like it costs anything at all. But when you figure, Fran, all the other things that are costing me fives and threes and twos—my gosh, it's a wonder I have enough to eat and smoke a cigarette."

"Well, how else you going to see me, when she gets here." Fran had pulled him aside, away from the prying ears of Big Joe. "It sure is going to make it easier for us to get together if you have a car that you can just hop into."

She looked up at him, her eyes clear as a lake. Leroy looked into those eyes and saw his future in them. Fran was right; without the car he'd have no chance to see her. He thought of the winter ahead, of how the back seat of a big car, with the windows closed tight and the rain pouring down in thick, foglike sheets, became almost as perfect for love-making as the most expensive suite in the fanciest hotel. And a lot more cozily intimate, too. Sure enough, he'd take the big bus of a Buick.

"Okay, Fran, but, remember—it's for us, so's we can be together."

"Sure, hon, you know that's the way it's gonna be."

Leroy showed his driver's license, signed a form, and the car was his. Fran stood by his side, her face rather vacant. Leroy glanced at her and presumed that she was lost in a dream of their soon being together.

The truth of it was that she was making a rapid calculation of how much commission Big Joe was going to give her on this new deal. Thinking of money always gave Fran that dreamy look.

"How about a nice long ride, Fran?" Leroy said gaily as he started to drive the Buick in and around the neighborhood.

"Now don't go putting off that house-renting chore, Leroy," Fran said, her voice teasing. "You're in a spending mood and I don't want to let you go before it fades away." She playfully slapped his wrist as she gave her orders to him.

Glumly, Leroy drove out toward the highway, hurt because Fran had not referred to the house as "our" house, though he knew well enough it was actually for Edna and him.

The inevitable was staring him right in the face, and, as a man, he had to face it back, stare it down.

"The house I have in mind is out on Sherman Road. Just pure luck I stumbled on it. You're going to really love this one."

Fran knew she had him hooked now. He wouldn't complain about the money. He had had her, and he would want her again. Well, he'd pay for it—but plenty!

" … and the rent is only eighty a month. Isn't that a steal? Of course, there's fifty dollars you have to pay as a bonus for getting such a buy. Make out the check to me, and I'll give it to my friend who steered me to this house. Okay?"

Then and there Leroy wanted to shout "Enough," but a car swerved toward him from the side. By the time he had maneuvered the Buick back on the lane, the right moment seemed to have passed.

But his anger, his sense of frustration, his choked rage did not pass. Perhaps sensing his sullenness, Fran placed her hand lightly along his outer thigh. Gently she massaged as she reassured him of her affection for him. Controlling his desire, he moved his leg away from her. She sat back, smiling more to herself than for him.

"Don't think I'm pushing you, Leroy, baby. But I just want us to be together so-o-o much."

Leroy took one hand from the wheel and threw it around Fran's shoulder. She nestled close to him, giving him driving directions. In a few minutes they came to the block she had in mind.

The neighborhood had the air of so many dingy, furnished rooms expanded into cottages and set out on the road for everyone to stare at their dilapidated state. The tiny front patches of grass had an unkempt, straggly look. Clotheslines fluttered, filled with cheap, sleazy trousers and shirts. The rows and rows of doll-like houses were exactly the same. In the heat of the afternoon the streets were deserted, and the development had the air of a ghost town, the slum part of a ghost town. Paint was peeling from the clapboard. The curtains were gray with dust. In the summer air was the smell of rancid butter.

They parked the Buick at the corner and walked slowly up the block. Idly Leroy wondered which of the houses was for sale. They all had the same look of abandoned decay.

At number forty-four they stopped. Fran led Leroy up the sloping, rotting two steps that were attached to the front porch. The front door was unlocked. Gloomily, Leroy followed her in.

The first ugly feature of the house that hit him was the garish wallpaper. A turquoise background was littered with coral and lemon-colored flowers. His eyes stung and swam before him.

The floor creaked. Across it scurried a brown field rat. The fireplace was stuffed with garbage and old rags. A breeze came up and the windows rattled in their casements. Another glorified outhouse, he thought.

Fran, calling to him from the one, undersized bedroom, shouted, "Leroy, I bet your Edna would love this place."

For just a second, Leroy was stunned. And then he regained his senses, for, he knew, Fran was right. He too was sure that Edna would think this a palace compared to what she had known. It had a boiler, three whole rooms, plus a tiny dining area, and a full utility kitchen.

The fact of the matter was that it was, for him, too, the best home he had ever had the chance to live in. Then why was he so depressed with it? Inside himself, Leroy knew. He had envisioned this house with Fran in it—not Edna. And for Fran it would not do at all. But, he reasoned as he set his mind on the right track again, it was Edna who was his wife, the woman who would be here.

He walked outside and sat down on the sagging porch. Fran came out, too, and sat down beside him. As he wrote in his checkbook, he said, rather wistfully, "I guess this means we won't be seeing each other too much—if any. I mean, now that I got a house and Edna coming up here to live, and—"

"Don't be silly, silly," Fran said, quickly kissing him behind his ear. "You ain't seen the last of me. My gosh, you don't want to live in an abandoned house, do you? 'Course not. Now, first off, you'll need some basic pieces of furniture, an' a new gas range, refrigerator, an'—"

As she went on, Leroy heard, in the back of his mind, Sailor's accusation against Fran. "She's gypped every bastard in the shop." But he looked at her and did not hear that hating voice again. He saw only a lovely, cleanlooking, sweetly perfumed woman who spent much of her time with him, kept him from loneliness, gave him her very body and every favor she knew how to bestow.

"Let's get to the agent and make it official," Leroy said, jumping to his feet. Fran caught up his hand and led him a few doors up.

The agent's office was a slightly enlarged telephone booth with a fly-specked window, on which was clumsily painted a sign that read *Loans—Real Estate—Insurance.*

Inside, a short, squat blob of a man, looking like a human pimple, reclined in a tip-back swivel chair. It seemed as though he were just dumped there.

"Hiya, Fran. What's new? This your friend, the guy you say gets the house?"

"Sure thing, Freddie. This is Leroy Landers, a real swell guy. He'll move in right away, and, believe me, you're getting a terrific tenant."

"Good enough for me, whatever you say. They've been driving me crazy trying to rent that house." He stood up to shake Leroy's hand.

He accepted Leroy's check for the first month's rent and peeled off two twenties and gave it to Fran. Leroy was surprised that she took it. He wondered how much the furniture and appliances were going to cost. When he would get home that night, he would check into his money situation. It filled him with a sense of dread.

The farm he had once so vividly dreamed of was now just a fading, hard-to-remember memory. A new dream, one in which Fran shone as brightly as the starriest ornament in the heavens, had replaced it. Whatever he now desired had as its main appeal, Fran; she had moved into the very center of his life, and all his actions came from her wishes, her commands.

"Look at him, Freddie!" Fran said sharply, pointing to Leroy. "He gets practically—for him, at least—what is a mansion, and he stands there looking like the atom bomb is going to explode on his head."

"Lissen, Mr. Landers," Freddie said, dumping himself back on the chair. "If you want to back out … "

Leroy grabbed Fran and stormed out of the office, glaring angrily at Freddie. He hated to be talked about as though he were a prize bull at a county fair. These glib city people had no respect for a man's pride or dignity.

In order to prevent him from exploring the shabby neighborhood, Fran immediately suggested that they go on to Eddie's for a couple of beers. Leroy was quick to agree.

They chose a quiet table, off in a corner, and listened to the love songs being shouted from the crazy-colored jukebox.

"Them words make sense, you know, Fran," Leroy said, holding her hand. "I used to think that all those love songs were the same, but they're not. When youyou care about a—person, they—they seem to be a special message written for you."

"Now, Leroy. You know that—"

Fran's efforts to change the subject were greatly aided by the entrance of three of Sailor's buddies. As they went on to their own table, they purposely pushed Leroy against the wall. He sprang to his feet, fists clenched.

"Forget it, Leroy, you've shown 'em all already. They weren't looking for real trouble, just being snotty."

"I know—but that's the way everyone is. Even the guys who did talk to me—they don't speak to me none now at all."

Fran nodded quietly. "It figures."

"It does? How come?" Leroy looked up with interest.

"Well, it's something like this," Fran said, struggling for a simple, easily understood explanation. "Up here, fist fights are a sort of game. They're more or less imitations of these scraps the fellows see on television or at the Golden Gloves. They wind up with a couple of black eyes or a busted nose, and they're forgotten after a couple of days or so. But crippling a guy's back so he can't work for maybe six months—that's something else again."

Leroy was bewildered and showed it. But stubborn, too. The sudden set of his jaw revealed his refusal to accept the idea of fighting as any sort of game.

"He got off lucky. Down home, I'd have stomped his ribs in, too."

"That's just it, Leroy. You aren't down home now. Neither am I, nor thousands of other hillbillies. And most of us'll never go home again. Neither will we ever be at home here. Most of these guys' fathers and mothers were born in the old country, but to them, we're the foreigners. There are too many of us competing for jobs and houses and other things they want. The war-time boom is slackening, and they're beginning to be afraid we'll get in ahead of them. Your fight with Sailor just gave 'em an excuse to take their feelings out on you. They'll hate your guts from here on out—and mostly because to them you'll represent all the hillbillies rolled into one. It's exactly the same treatment you rednecks gave the niggers down South."

Suddenly Leroy's yearning to escape renewed itself. When he had climbed aboard the Power-Trak bus to come North, he certainly hadn't anticipated any such maze of complications in his life.

It shouldn't be too difficult to snatch up his few belongings, jump in the car and head for home. But even as the thought occurred to him, he knew he could never do it. It was impossible for him to go back now.

"The worst of it is, Leroy," Fran continued, "you're stuck with it. And there isn't a thing you can do about it. You can't go back. Some can and do, but you're not that type."

Leroy jerked out of his reverie, startled to find Fran apparently reading his mind.

"I don't bother none of them," he blurted. "An' they better not bother me. I'm stayin'. Oh, I'll go back for Edna—some day, but later I'll stay on."

A sudden fear gripped Fran. With Leroy in a fighting mood, hating the unfriendly city people around him, he might not want to go ahead furnishing his newly rented house.

His sharp aggressiveness provoked her anger and her cunning. She would have to work on him, convince him that he still needed her, and that only by staying would he remain within touching distance.

For a moment she sat watching a young couple dancing cheek-to-cheek. If only the clumsy ape danced, she thought, I could work on him here. But at least he has that car.

"Look, Leroy, before you beat everyone in sight to death, let's get out of here. Let's go for a drive—honey."

That one word of endearment was a command for Leroy, and out they went as quickly as the check was paid.

The air had a suggestion of autumn chill in it, and when they settled themselves in the car, Fran moved close to Leroy. Her fingers running along the outside of his thigh and her tongue darting deliciously in the contours of his ear evoked in Leroy the memory of their passion together.

Resolutely attentive to his driving, he continued staring ahead, not permitting himself to throw one arm around Fran. Finally, to avoid saying foolishly romantic things, he broke the silence.

"Why did you tell the agent I'll be moving right in, Fran? Edna won't be here for some time."

"Just write and tell her to come on up on the bus, that's all."

Fran uttered her words slowly, carefully, watching Leroy's face with much concern. She could not push him too far. Quite obviously Leroy resented being forced to commit himself to a line of continuous action—the rental of the house and all the items he'd have to purchase for it. Most important, it meant that Edna would be returning, and that his sneaking around with Fran would have to end—or at least be sharply cut down.

"Okay, Fran," Leroy said, his glance straying to her face, absorbed now in silent scheming. "I'll write tomorrow and mention it."

Fran recognized this as just another stalling device. Leroy would suggest that Edna come on up next spring. By that time, Fran fervently hoped, she would be in California enjoying the sun, the swimming and some man she really wanted. The idea was to get Edna up here as quickly as possible, and to get those appliances ordered.

Leroy lapsed into silence, and Fran decided to let the subject rest until a more advantageous moment. There were ways to deal with Leroy's sullen stubbornness—and Fran knew them all.

"Let's go on to the carnival at Riverview, Leroy. They'll be closing up soon."

In the distance, the sideshow fairyland glowed with its gaudy lights, circus colors, and the noise of hundreds of suckers being happily fleeced of their money.

The midway was crowded with college kids and oldsters off for a mad whirl. Fran stuck close to Leroy, waiting and watching to see when the bitterness in his mood would ebb. When she saw a relaxation of his facial muscles, she steered him to the shooting gallery.

Leroy's face was one huge smile of innocent delight as he spent six dollars at the range. For his money he won a huge Panda, which he lovingly bestowed on Fran. His aim was still country-perfect, and his pride and self-respect zoomed to astronomical heights.

Seeing his eyes glittering with triumph, Fran knew that the moment had come to make her move. Taking his elbow with unusual possessiveness, she led him firmly toward the Caterpillar, the local version of the tunnel of love. The small, green-hooded cars twisted sinuously through a dark lagoon, the walls of which were covered with pictures of men and women in tender embraces.

They got in line in back of a dreamy couple who seemed to float past the ticket taker.

"I hope you don't mind me being forward with you, Leroy. But I did want to go on this ride—with you. I must say I've been here before, but never in there with a man."

Her lie was hidden under the wistful lowering of her eyelashes.

When they entered, they found the seat still warm from the previous occupants. Leroy sat carefully on his half of the seat and did not draw Fran close. As the cars began to glide snakelike through the water, Fran reached behind her and drew the green hood over them. Total darkness enveloped them.

She whispered, "I've never seen it so totally dark, Leroy. It's kind of scary."

Leroy put an arm stiffly around Fran's waist. She touched it, lifted it and cupped it tightly over her breast. His palm slid over her breast slowly. Fran searched for his lips, found them and began to kiss them fervently. Her tongue explored the innermost recesses of his mouth. She could feel Leroy strain towards her, surrounding her with his massive strength. His other hand slipped under her skirt and his fingers danced on her bare flesh. Fran stroked Leroy idly behind his ear. Along his neck the skin burned with rising desire.

Then the green hoods automatically fell back and the car rode slowly out of the artificial lagoon.

They broke their embrace suddenly, and almost without knowing how he got there, Leroy found himself by her side, walking as if on stilts.

Fran looked up at him and laughed, not in happiness over their mutual give-and-take pleasure, but at the frustrated anguish in Leroy's eyes.

She was somewhat startled to see him move toward the ticket booth again.

"Oh, no you don't, you tiger. No more tonight. You're a little too rough and eager for me."

"Oh, hell, that was the shortest damn ride."

"Good thing it wasn't any longer, you Rover Boy—else I'd had to have walked back."

Leroy puffed up his chest with masculine pride. His eyes were narrow with delight, and so he missed the coldly appraising look Fran sent his way.

A big overgrown boy, she thought. But not much of a man.

After a few minutes of driving, Leroy wanted her again. He pulled the car sharply into a little retreat. He drew her to him and, before he began to touch her, his body thrilled, trembled in anticipation of her never-ending capacity to arouse him. Around them a moon glowed like a white-hot opal in the sky.

Leroy began to fumble for her knees, remembering the silky excitement of her nyloned stocking and the satiny flesh beyond.

Fran pushed him firmly away.

"Cut it out, you big goon. No more of that till you come back home. Don't bother writing and stalling some more. Just you go down there and bring her back."

"But with Edna here—"

"I know—darling. But we're not going to take her everywhere we go, are we?" Her voice was an anguished plea.

In a very real way this was like arousing him, Fran thought to herself. Only instead of touching or probing along his body, she would simply speak or smile in a certain way. The end result would be the same—capitulation to *her* desires.

"How can I get a leave from the plant so quickly. And—"

"They're not going to put up a fuss. They need men too much. Just say Edna's sick and you're taking her up here for a good doctor to look her over."

"I—"

"Don't even go back to the plant at all. I'm in personnel. I'll take care of everything."

"But what happens when we get back? Just can't move into an empty house. Even Edna likes to sleep on a bed and eat out of plates."

"No worry, honey. I'll get off tomorrow and get the essentials. Soon as you leave, I'll start shopping. You'll have everything in your house, ready to use, when you come in for the first time."

Leroy sat thoughtful for a minute. The way he'd been scrimping, even on his meals, to build up a nest egg. Hard savings he'd planned not to touch for a long time. He leaned over to look at her face.

"And you, will you be there to greet me when I come in for the first time?"

"What the—Why shouldn't I?"

A tremor of fear ran through Fran. Of course it was only the wildest of lucky guesses that Leroy had chanced upon. But suppose it was an unlucky omen. Maybe it meant that her plan to duck out wouldn't work as she had planned it. No. That kind of talk was crazy.

"I don't know. I just thought you was brushing me off, Fran, and I—"

"What's eating you, Leroy?" She waited for a response, but, instead, he stared off into the darkness. "I thought that after we— you—after we had made love together like we did, we'd be close forever. I mean that, or else I wouldn't have suggested seeing you after Edna comes back. But if you don't trust me, maybe we'd better break it off right now."

Like an artist spreading paint across his canvas in a certain color calculated to shock or please or excite, Fran put a smile of feigned dismay and hopelessness across her face.

Leroy drew her to him again. "It's something Sailor said one time. Been kinda pesterin' me all along."

"That big ape has been so jealous he might tell any kind of damn lie. What was it?"

"He claims you're married to a guy in the pen. How come you never said anything about it?"

"Oh, for crissakes. Is that all? I figured you knew all about it," she lied. "Everyone else does. Don't expect me to talk about it; I'm trying to forget it." Fran shuddered painfully as though racked with memories of a horrifying past. "Everything's over between us—Stan and me. He won't be back for years, and I can get a divorce anytime I want it—because of him being a convict."

"How come you didn't?"

"Never had any reason to—up till now. Just been waiting for somebody else to come along, I guess—if they ever do," Fran sobbed, throwing herself into his arms. "The lawyers want two hundred dollars to take care of it, anyway. I haven't been able to get it together-taking care of Ma and all. Oh, I don't know what to do."

Leroy snapped on the panel lights and Fran demurely drew down her skirts. She saw Leroy fumbling with his open check-book on his knees.

"How much you need for them things for the house?"

"Oh, about five hundred, I guess," Fran quavered.

Leroy straightened, looked thoughtfully off into the darkness.

"Or just make it four hunderd." Fran hastily amended. "That'll be enough for you to start on."

Leroy bent to his scribbling again. "I'm putting that other two hundred on here too," he said. "Better see yourself a lawyer right away."

Fran threw herself at him impulsively, overwhelming him with affection, but thoughtfully protecting the check he thrust into her hand, lest it be crushed.

"Now—" she whispered breathlessly as she drew away, "that's all till you get back. Please—please don't keep me waiting. I want you a part of me—like it was before-real soon."

CHAPTER SEVEN

OR A second or so, Fran permitted herself almost to believe what she had ardently whispered to Leroy. Then a cold, calculating chill of reason, so strong it was almost a physical tightening in her body, gripped her and set her passion aside.

Leroy was in a dreamlike state as he drove her home. His only thought was to go back to his room, shower, dress and refuel the car to make the journey home. Presenting Edna to Fran would be proof of his faith in their relationship, evidence that he intended to be as honest as he could with Fran. When he thought of his previous doubts about her, he cursed himself for his suspicions. Fran was his, dearer to him than his own wife, more true to him than his own self-confidence and trust in his judgment.

The house was dark and quiet when Fran entered. Some of her mother's huge dresses were thrown about the living room, and Renie's heavily scented perfume hung to the stale, humid air. As she made her way to her room, Fran could hear Chunky's heavy breathing, sputtering like leaky plumbing, from behind his barred door. Maybe it was those hormone pills that gave him the energy to sleep so hard, she thought mirthlessly.

Her room had obviously been cleaned. New curtains fluttered lightly at the windows. The furniture smelled faintly of polish. Sophie had put on her dresser a picture of Stan. It had been taken at the beach just before they were married. They both wore matching bikinis. Side by side, they were a study in health and animal lustiness.

As she undressed before it, Stan seemed to step out of the photograph and enter her hidden thoughts. Fran began to recapture the touch of his caress against her. But in another moment she remembered, too, the painful slap of his open palm one night when she had complained that she was too tired to make love to him. At times he would be tender to an almost poetical intensity; other times, though, his savagery was a series of violences upon her.

Men had become frightening but tempting creatures for Fran. In the few years since Stan had been put away, they had come to be only instruments of her pleasure, and that pleasure was only physical, a sensual, volcanic experience that never touched her affections. She took no joy in deliriously exciting her partner; no real enjoyment in her own cataclysms of desire. She existed merely as the repository partner in a futile, occasionally titillating encounter. Sometimes in the moments of her ecstasy she wanted to dig her nails deep into their backs, hoping to pierce through to their surprised hearts and stab them to death. And then, in another time, just after the tumult had died down, she would laugh at them as creatures less than human, whose only reason for existence was that they carried with them certain sexual equipment capable of pleasing her. The basic question of whether she was ever really pleased never troubled Fran for she never dared to think about it. She saw all men as great brutal children and realized that she was in a position, by simply being a lovely woman, of frustrating their childish sport with her by holding back everything from them but the sexual terrain of her body. In this way she was conqueror, but she had never known what it was to submit in delicious capture. She had every physical and sensual quality of womanliness, but her soul had never grasped the core of her femininity. Emotionally, she was as untouched sexually as the most sheltered virgin, for she had never known a man as a human being—only a perpetrator of cruelty or a recipient of her silent scorn.

She was as locked up inside as surely as Stan was encased in a cell. But she hoped to love again, not some aged object of pity like Chunky, or some witless boy like Leroy, but a man of consequence and determination. When she prayed at all, she prayed to meet this man. The money she earned by hook and crook she hoped would buy her way into a world where these men abounded. It was the justification for her very existence, for without its reality as a goal, she would be completely without illusions and, therefore, entirely at the mercy of totally demoralizing cynicism.

Fran entered her world of sleep in a frenzy of planning. *Stan would be out soon. How much money did she have saved? She would have to look. Leroy was certainly hooked, but good! Now to take control of the situation when Edna got back. If she was still here. And old Chunky—she'd have to be easier on him when he tried to make her again. When would he try? When…?*

Her plans half-made, her emotions half-realized, Fran descended into the formless, black eternity of sleep.

Leroy carried out his plans just as he'd made them. Thirty-six hours and five quarts of oil later he was in Rock Slide, Arkansas. Home. The Buick was dusty, but he knew the home folks would sure be impressed.

Near the post office he stopped the car and got out. The smell of his homeland rushed up to meet him like a welcoming friend. The aroma of the city streets, stale and raspy in the throat, faded, overcome by the scent of wild roses and fern. Nearby Leroy heard the light laughter of a stream. He walked to it, knelt, and drank deeply from its bright, sun-glinted water. He stripped his shirt from his tired, over-traveled body and doused his face and chest with the refreshing water.

Alive again in the old familiar way of his boyhood, he got back into the Buick and drove to his farm. He drove past the red-scarred hills and around the mossy glens. Fran had said to hurry, and her words were like added horsepower to his car.

First he stopped at his Uncle Val's house. Young Tad, no more than seven years of age, ran out to greet him, full of pride in his new role of host and head of the house.

"How about a nice, cool dipper of spring water, Uncle Leroy?" the boy said, waving Leroy to sit by him on the porch steps.

"Fine, Tad, fine. But where's your pa?"

"Off to preaching school."

"And where's your Aunt Edna?"

"Where she always is nowadays. Off at the fishin' pond. Goes up three times a week regular. And doesn't even ask to take me along. I like catfishin', too."

Leroy was mildly shocked to hear Tad tell of Edna's sudden interest in privacy and fishing.

"I followed her once, but she caught me and wouldn't let me stay. Want me to show you where?"

"No, boy, I'll find it out myself, I'm sure."

Tad got up from the porch and went back into the house, disappointed at not being asked along. That city sure rubbed off his family feelin', Tad thought as he went back in the house. As he turned, Leroy was walking determinedly back on the road.

The sun flashed on the water, making it dance and sparkle like so many jewels. The sound of summer filled Leroy's ears with an old, familiar tune—of birds, of rushing water, of the leaves rustling slightly in the light breeze.

He walked the paths into the woods slowly, savoring each site from his childhood as he would a sip of rare wine. The trees seemed to nod to him a motion of welcome. So absorbed in the landscape was he that Leroy almost failed to notice the bit of white cloth fluttering on the luxuriant emerald grass.

When he did realize what it was, he was struck with the fact that it was a picnic setting for two, including two fishing poles stuck firmly in the ground. A man's shirt flew from one pole; one of Edna's blouses served as a flag for the other.

Nearby he heard the murmuring lapping of the water. It was the lake slapping gently against a rowboat moored about twenty feet down the shore.

Silence surrounded him like a weight. Suddenly footsteps were heard, and Edna appeared, breathlessly, an eager smile garishly painted across her face.

"Leroy! Leroy, darlin'!"

Eagerly she threw herself into Leroy's automatically outstretched arms. Between quick, stinging kisses, Edna's laugh giggled nervously. Leroy said nothing, but permitted himself to be led away from the picnic site. Edna's grip was a little too steady, as if he were a great, bulky encumbrance that had to be steered into safety.

When that white patch was almost out of sight, Leroy halted, turned and faced it.

"Expectin' a friend, Edna?" he said. His eyes searched her face. What he saw gave weight to his suspicions. Her lipstick was smeared. The bra section of her bathing suit was sloppily adjusted. Her hair was straggly and looser than she had usually combed it.

"Not any more, Leroy," Edna giggled. "Tad was here. Always comes catfishin' with me. But he run off. Got bored, I guess."

"That shirt ain't Tad's."

"Oh, but it sure is Tad's idea. See, that's his daddy's shirt, and he kinda likes to think of it as a flag and that we're explorers here."

Again Edna giggled, and Leroy hated himself for ever thinking that childish habit cute. But Edna's facility at lying with a straight face certainly wasn't childish. Even when Leroy tried to pierce her gaze, she stared him down until he was forced to turn away.

"O.K. Let's get going," Leroy said, steering her back to the picnic blanket.

Together they scooped up the picnic remains and went toward the cabin. Along the way Leroy cursed himself for not striking Edna, for not there and then dissolving the mockery that their marriage had become. And then he wanted Edna, not in passion or in tenderness, but simply as a body to punish with lusting brutality.

The cabin was deserted when they arrived. Edna slumped heavily in a chair. Leroy noticed that her breasts had begun to sag and that slight folds of fat had begun to form under her chin. Her hair was unkempt and coarse-looking. Edna had let herself go, and Leroy hated her for doing so.

He went over to her and she raised her face to his for a kiss, but instead he just stared, wondering who she really was and what she now meant to him. An odor of the farmland settled invisibly around her. She had become a sexless, almost unwomanly creature.

Edna threw one arm around Leroy's neck and drew him close to her. "You know, I almost forgot what it was like to bed with you, Leroy. Almost, but not quite—"

With an air of a young girl about her, she rose from the chair and went to the bed. She lay down on it and rolled her arms and legs about; her body struck abandoned poses. The extra flesh on her thighs and upper arms trembled. Her skirt billowed up her thighs. When she had changed out of her bathing suit, she had put nothing on under her skirt.

He turned away and went to the window to draw the shade.

Edna's wheezy breathing filled the room. Behind him, Leroy could hear her rustling and moving. He knew that she would be naked when he could turn around.

For just a second he stood by the window, watching the little lake ripple by. At first the water appeared uninhabited. Then Leroy heard the rowboat. It was being rowed slowly, carefully, as if to be able to make itself suddenly disappear at a moment's notice. The rower used every advantage to stay close to shore, out of sight. The boat twisted in and out of the muddy banks and overhanging trees, a serpent among the reeds.

As it curved along a contour that dipped near Leroy's cabin, the identity of the rower became immediately apparent. This was a man named Hap Cullen, a man he had known all his life. So had Edna. And now Leroy had the feeling that Edna knew him about as intimately as a woman could know a man.

Hap was the only serious rival Leroy ever had for Edna. He was a handsome man, dark-colored, with long sideburns and a sullen, almost leering twist to his lips. He was the hill musician, dancer, jokester, and, it was said, local stud. The story was that he would have sex with any living creature, providing that the creature was a female of the species. Though it had to be admitted that he liked female humans best of all.

Hap rowed past the house and Leroy turned away from the window. He could leave her now, right now. Her body lay waiting for him, already aroused with desire. If he walked off now, some other man, Hap Cullen most probably, would take his place. In the dark, in her passion, she would never know the difference. And later it wouldn't matter anyway.

But even as he thought of it, even as his thoughts eased the weight of his enslavement to her, lifted it off his shoulders, he knew he couldn't go through with it. His will was weak, his self-assertion weaker still. Events with Fran had proven to him that he could not act until bitter circumstance ganged up on him and *forced* him to a desperate decision. And desperate was not quite the way he felt. He felt trapped and bitter and helpless, but still Fran remained in his heart as a relief to his pain.

In a rage and helpless self-pity he turned again to Edna. Slowly he went to her and fell against her flabby, heaving body. At first his passion spread slowly through him, as if his desire was dragged by heavy chains. And then the bitterness turned to malevolent intensity. Her body became an object of attack by him. Fighting, surging restlessly, floundering against her flesh, he thrashed about in his own futility, hurting her and punishing himself for the entrapping net life had spun around him. The moment of climax came for him as a final, almost fatal blow. And then his courage failed him as his virility ebbed out of his body. Almost sobbing, he fell upon her body, not aware of his identity or hers, but only that at least she was a human being under him, a heart to cushion his agony. The sea of ineffectuality that was his existence swallowed him and he drowned in a storm-tossed sleep.

When he awoke it was evening. In the other room he heard the voices of his family, but his senses were full of the fetid, unwashed odor of Edna. Her body folded itself too closely against his. Her bulk seemed to suffocate him. Her lust had turned to insatiable greed, and there was no real desire to please her. His only thoughts were of Fran, of her delicacy and fire, and the warmth of her giving body during their night of love together.

He stood in the doorway of their darkened room, looking out into the other room of their shanty. This was grinding poverty here, a truly animal existence. No matter how shabby their home was in the factory town, it was a great deal better than this. As much as Leroy had wanted to escape Power-Trak and all the hostility and frustration there, he wanted to return now to at least the status of a human being. Away from Fran he was like a lost soul far away from the fire of care and love.

Sadly, he went back to bed and waited sleeplessly for the morning and the long ride back, not alone, but truly isolated, as he would be going back with his wife, a woman he did not love—to a woman he feared did not love him at all, but one to whom he now knew he was helplessly bound.

In the morning all went well. The family was properly sorry to see him go back so soon; Edna was adequately eager to try city life; he was just mildly depressed.

Even the fact that Hap Cullen had asked—with absolute gall, Leroy thought—to be taken along, did not disturb Leroy. There would be a job for Hap, and Power-Trak was a big place; there was no need for them running into each other.

Edna tried not to show too much interest in Hap as a passenger, but Leroy could see them holding hands and nestling a bit too close to each other in the back seat.

Screw 'em, Leroy thought. Screw 'em both. If Edna wants to get off my back and under Hap—well, let her. But his bravado was completely false. He knew that he would kill Hap Cullen if he ever caught them together. Kill Hap and then kill Edna. Whatever he did, or she did on the side, Edna was still his wife and owed him loyalty. He would wear her like a heavy chain around his neck and love her as a convict learns to love his shackles. She was his wife—not his woman, but his wife—and as such she was to be protected—as much as any object he owned would have to be protected.

And after a while he didn't look back in the rearview mirror. Not even when Edna would giggle quietly and Hap would be silent, with only his breathing rising excitedly in the wind across the long trip home.

CHAPTER EIGHT

F RAN waited two weeks before she decided it was time to see
Leroy. During these weeks she was not entirely unaware
of his actions. She knew he would figure she was giving him a
chance to get settled. And as it happened, Hap Cullen and she
had struck up a chance acquaintance at a birthday party for one
of the fellows in Hap's shop at Power-Trak. The fact that they
both knew Leroy started their relationship; overpowering physical attraction for one another quickly consolidated it.

In Hap, Fran found the almost perfect man. The last thing
Hap wanted was a binding relationship, and yet he was able to
communicate through his love-making alone a very real, satisfying "presence." It sufficed for Fran; it almost gave her pleasure.
She found Hap frenzied and tireless in bed, a casual friend in
other situations. But like most of her twisted relationships, this
affair with Hap, because it was so rewarding, threatened Fran
with fears of the future: it would have to end—somehow, someday—and she would be left dependent on a man who did not
need her anymore.

But she would think of that another day. Right now she
was inveigling Hap into the same pay-as-you-go deal that had
entrapped Leroy so neatly. Hap wasn't a family man; so he didn't
plan to buy too many appliances, but he loved lots of clothes, and
Fran preyed and played on his vanity so that he bought suit after
suit at her suggestion.

She had been with Hap last night, and after their sex together,
Hap mentioned how his old pal Leroy sure would envy him now.

Fran was a bit frightened. Any other man except Leroy would take the hint, find himself another gal to play around with; but not Leroy. According to Hap, he was still searching the corridors at Power-Trak for her, hoping to pick up again where they had left off. What was with that hillbilly boy, Fran thought. She decided then to do something drastic, something that would end forever his pestering insistence.

Fran had another man. And she had him good—right where she wanted him—right where he didn't know he could be had!

"Oh, *there* you are! Hi, Leroy. Where you been keeping yourself?" Fran approached Leroy waving a cutely crooked finger at him, a mock chastisement, complete with calculated frown and batted eyelashes.

"I? Where *I've* been keeping myself. Listen, Fran—"

"Oh, I know, Leroy, honey. But I had to change jobs with a woman who got sick, and—and anyway now we're together."

Leroy fidgeted with his work cap. A torrent of reproach rushed to his lips, but the sight of Fran with a warm smile for him, for him alone, dammed them as surely as a steel wall.

"You call this talkin' here 'together'?"

"Well, I know we ain't been together like you must mean for a long time now, but we will soon. You'll see—we'll all be together very soon now."

Involuntarily the actress in Fran spaced the words out in a measured, melodramatic fashion. But it all went over the head of Leroy, who was still busy feasting on the idea of standing here talking to Fran.

"Everything all right with the stuff I picked out for you and Edna? I'm dyin' to come out to the house and see how it all looks."

"It's all fine, Fran. Real nice, like you say."

Leroy remembered then that, along with the cheap, gaudy furniture and appliances, he found a drawerful of time payment books. Singly they were just a dollar or two here and there. But Leroy still hadn't summoned up enough nerve to total them. All he knew was that he hardly had anything left over at the end of the week, and the few bucks that remained, Edna soon frittered away. The Big Dream of the farm and new tractor equipment and arable land—that all was just a painful memory.

"I was just thinkin' about the two hundred I give you for the lawyer's fee so that you and Stan can get the divorce over with. What's happened on that score, Fran?"

"Oh, that," Fran replied airily, with a slight wave of her hand. "We're gonna have to wait on that. My lawyer's out of town on another case. He oughta be back soon. Don't worry, Leroy, the money's safe."

There was a lot of real truth in that remark. Because the money was safe—safe in a deposit box in the local bank. No lawyer had seen a dollar of it—or would.

"You can trust me, Leroy. And if you don't, why, your pal Hap Cullen'd make sure I didn't get away with anything. Don't think I haven't heard all about your doings from him. I sort of met him around here and now he's living with Ma and me. A real nice guy."

She said the speech quickly, not daring to give Leroy a chance to interrupt. The look on Leroy's face when she mentioned Hap convinced her that there was no love lost between them. They might be neighbors back in Rock Slide, but here at Power-Trak they were enemies, and for reasons not entirely known to either of them. It gave sense of power to Fran to be the manipulator of these two brawny men, both solid and raging strong. This sense of power went to her head, and she was inwardly laughing at the triumph of her schemes and at Leroy's oafish, unmanly stupidity.

"No, we can't see each other this Saturday at the company dance—I'll be out of town on business," she said defiantly. "But I'll get in touch with you real soon. You wait and see."

Leroy reached out to hold her a second, but she eluded his grasp and strode vigorously away. He stood there a moment trying to recapture the exact inflection of her voice so that he could extract some measure of comfort from her indefinite promise. And then, ashamed of his begging, dependent manner, he shuffled back to his shop.

But he could not work. The thought that she had lied to him, that she might not be going to be out of town the night of the dance, haunted him, almost maddened him, with fearful insecurity.

He would go. He would *have* to go. If she was there, he would confront her with her deliberate deceit. Perhaps then she would, by her brazen callousness, free him from the spineless need he had developed for her. For if he saw her there, actually dancing in the arms of another man, then he knew he would have the courage to flaunt her dishonor and faithlessness to her face. She could have nothing but respect for him after that; the new spirit of resolution and defiance would win her over to him.

At home, Leroy found Edna curled up in bed with a box of cherry cream chocolates and a pile of movie romance magazines. The house had not been swept for days. Grime was already beginning to form on the windows. In the living room, the television blared on to a nonexistent audience.

"Where's my white shirts, you fat ox?" Leroy screamed at Edna. "Don't you ever pick your fat ass up out of that bed?"

"I jes' didn't get around to ironin' yet, Leroy. This is a big house, needs a lot of work."

His first thought was to run out and buy a brand new white shirt, but the four dollars it would cost would just not give him enough left over for tobacco for the rest of the week. He looked around him, at the shiny, showy-looking cheap furniture—more than he had ever owned in his whole life—and patted his stomach. Lately it was always just a little bit empty. Not that he was really hungry, but it came down to the fact that Edna bought the cheapest cuts of meat, and when he ate in a restaurant he watched the prices with special care. Sometimes, at moments of complete frustration such as this one, he had the uneasy feeling that Fran had bought him and sold him, body and soul.

Leroy found an old white shirt hanging in his closet. His suit had fallen to the floor. The amount of dust on it indicated how dirty the closet really was. Like a bull in silent rage, Leroy found a brush, dusted the suit and dressed quickly.

"Where you going, Leroy? Ain't you going to take me?"

"Quiet, you fat old bag. Just you go back and lie down and pop more chocolates into your gut."

"Leroy—!"

The slam of the front door drowned her tirade.

The room was crowded when Leroy entered the dance hall. Nevertheless, he saw Fran in the arms of a handsome stranger at once. Her eyes were closed, her body was pressed closely against the solid huskiness of the man. Her breath fluttered the hair above his left ear. She seemed to sway, almost float in heated proximity to his body.

Leroy's first impulse was to break in on them. But suddenly he knew that his action would accomplish nothing. The reverie Fran floated in abashed him. Her absorption in her partner, the blatant obviousness of her deception of Leroy—all conspired to silence his protest. The pain of his betrayal overwhelmed him, and the last remains of his manhood drained out of him as he turned and walked out of the dance hall.

Once outside he walked rapidly, though the vigor had left his rugged frame. Like a searing pain that would not abate, the realization grew in him that when he would see Fran again he would pretend not to have been here at all; a bit of strategy he knew she would not believe. She had come into his life like a long looked-for stranger, and now she was a sorceress, bewitching his existence, ruining him in hopeless subjection.

Anguished with these thoughts, Leroy walked for several hours. A light rain had fallen, and he wandered as if in a dream.

When he grew tired, he noticed that he was now almost full-circle back to where he started from. Compulsively he walked again to the entrance of the dance hall.

Fran had just walked down the steps and stood at the curb waiting for the stranger to hail a cab. She gazed after him adoringly, and, as they settled in the cab, Leroy noticed that she immediately nestled in his arms.

Wonder how long before he gets hooked to buy a car, Leroy thought as he watched the cab disappear into the night.

Despite his long walk, he was neither tired nor sleepy. He drove slowly home, a curious gnawing feeling spreading through him. He needed desperately an object on which to vent his frustration, the hurt of his rejection by Fran. He was, therefore, angry all over again to find the house dark when he pulled the car into the driveway.

Defeat enveloped him, choked him as he shuffled into the house. Immediately a half-strange, half-familiar odor attacked him; it was the stink of a cold cigar. And it was not long out—the darkness was sharp.

Slowly, on cat feet, he inched his way to the bedroom, crossed the threshold, and quickly jerked on the light.

Edna was in bed—alone. But her eyelids fluttered ever so faintly under the surprise of the bright light, and her breath came too heavily for real sleep.

He came to her, a hand ready to slap her mercilessly across her face, to go on beating her until he could hit no more. But as he bent over her, his face contorted with rage, he remembered his actions earlier in the evening. Right now where he wanted to be was in someone else's bed—near Fran. So why shouldn't Edna want to cheat? He realized now that she knew that their sex together had become a passionless, perfunctory thing. He gave nothing to her except the raw energy of his body, and she offered nothing but a flabby, emotionless shape.

Overcome by the mockery of their mutually destructive relationship, Leroy stumbled from the bedroom. Edna snored on. He made his way to the divan and lay staring at the ceiling until the thump of the Sunday paper announced the end of a wretched, tortured night.

Once, during the late hours of the night, Fran turned in her sleep and awoke for a moment. She had a terrible vision of Stan suddenly come back from the penitentiary. Near her, Tim lay like a deadweight. She remembered Leroy's bitter, almost tragic look as he saw them dance together. A wave of loneliness, something like a great tidal wave, rushed over her. No one, no one in the entire world, meant anything to her; she was as desolate as an orphan lost in a dark, cruel forest. The oppression of this realization swept through her with heavy, increasing rumbles of fear. As a drowning castaway would reach for a rope, she turned to the stranger near her in the darkness and searched for the secret touchstones of his desire. Sleepily, heavily, he turned to her, and in a few moments she lost her fears in the rush of his passion.

The morning was relentlessly honest. The shabby house was exposed in all its vulgarity. And so was Edna.

She made no attempt to wash in the morning. A stick of peppermint chewing gum popped in her mouth took the place of brushing her teeth. When she had scratched the sand of sleep out of her eyes, she turned away from Leroy and reached for a movie magazine.

"Ain't you going to clean yourself up?" Leroy asked, hardly able to believe her filthy personal habits.

"We ain't going anywhere. It's just Sunday. And since when are you such a dude?"

"Lord, you are a pig, Edna. What the hell happened to you?"

"You never mind me much now—you know what I mean—so's no real reason to keep myself purty."

"Don't you ever clean the place? Don't you want to live nice?"

"Aw, Leroy, it's only furniture..."

"And me, you don't take care of me like a wife should."

"Well, man, I just said that you don't take care of me like a husband should."

His stomach beginning to stir, his mind wretchedly aware of the trapped state he had run himself into, Leroy could think of nothing to do but to strike out. He sat up in bed, stared down at the puffy, grimy face of the woman he had once hungered for as he had for no other woman in his life, and slapped her once, twice ... again and again across her face.

She screamed loudly, and then she went into a kind of convulsive sobbing. She leaped from the bed to the other side of the room, the blanket wrapped Indian fashion around her.

"You crummy bastard! you lousy scum! Sure, beat your own wife, maybe kill your own kid!"

"What—!"

"You heard me, you crazy slut-chasin' bastard! I'm pregnant, and no matter how lousy you are in bed, this one sure is yours."

"Oh, no! You lyin' bitch! You ain't telling the truth!"

But as surely as he would feel the final tightening twist of a hangman's noose, he knew it was true. The blood thin and slow in his body, he fell against the pillows and half-collapsed into the misery around him, wishing now that he were dead and buried and rid of the grinding degradation that had become his life.

CHAPTER NINE

Fran puffed at her cigarette impatiently. Within a few moments Leroy would be here. Fran had tried to get him to leave her alone for a week now, but Leroy was persistent. She wondered what the devil was bothering him. She'd noted his urgency, his despondency, and she decided, finally, that the time had come to use the most drastic measures to make sure that she would be free of him.

Fran sat in the shabby living room of her run-down home, waiting for the cranky sound of Leroy's Buick to assail her ears. Her hair shimmered in the night light as it poured through the window. A small scream of irritation escaped her lips.

"*Will* you stop that damned rocking, Ma?"

Sophie just smiled and went on rocking. She had been sitting there almost philosophically examining her daughter. Aware of Fran's good taste in clothes, her efforts to improve her diction and posture and "air" about her, she was also aware of the fact that Fran had become a thoroughgoing, pedigree bitch. There was almost nothing she wouldn't do for a buck, Sophie thought; sometimes she decided that there wasn't anything she wouldn't do for *twenty* bucks—Fran being her daughter or not.

"Now let me be, Fran. You just stop that being irritable. Is Leroy comin' over? That why you're so worked up?"

"Yes," Fran said, sitting down forcefully on the sofa opposite Sophie. "That oaf has pestered me all week. And, anyway, I really did think it was about time we had a showdown—end it all."

"You're right, Fran. Fella from the sticks like him can be pretty rough, can flip their wigs and start a real ruckus."

"I got a way, Ma. I got a way that's gonna send him away from here but good!"

Things had gone too far already, Fran knew. Each time she passed him in the plant, she had seen the glitter in his eyes, felt the angry tension in his way with her. He pressed her harder and harder for news about her divorce proceedings. It had become more and more difficult to manufacture lies, excuses, stalling assurances that all would soon be well, that they would be together. Desperation dragged at the corners of his mouth, and at times he seemed to be at the verge of losing all his self-control—this past week especially. Fran feared to be alone with him, sensing the fury that his frustration and bitterness had created.

"What about his wife?" Sophie droned on. "Where is she when Leroy decides to take an evenin' off? And what about Stan? With his good behavior time off, he should be home any day now, and you know what he'd say if he come in and find a goof like Leroy around? He'd say 'Turn around and start running, 'cause I'm gonna shoot to kill.' "

"Quit that movie talk, Ma. I know what I'm doing."

What she really wanted to be doing, Fran thought, was to be on a plane out of town. But her decision to leave after Leroy settled Edna down in the new house had been reversed. Too many profitable deals; too many gullible, city-dazed young hill country boys who never owned a radio and who wanted to buy the best. And then there was Chunky's hidden treasure chest of money. It was somewhere in the house; she knew it. But since that night she'd humiliated Chunky, the old man had not returned. She would make one more effort to get it—one real good one; get it and clear out before Stan got back. Everything would be for nothing if that bastard got back and took it all away from her—and he would, too.

She went to the window, impatient now with her waiting. From the bus stop she saw what had become a familiar figure approaching the house. It was not Leroy; it was his wife, Edna. Her figure was heavily bundled in a gaudy-colored, sleazy cloth coat. Almost furtively she made her way to the staircase and began to climb.

This was too good to be true, Fran thought. It was almost planned—Edna here now to meet Hap Cullen. What would Leroy say if he actually saw her in the—

The rains had come, bitter, heavy, and almost like weapons the drops hit the sidewalk. As though from behind a sheet of this water strafing from the sky, Leroy appeared.

Fran watched him park and then motioned Sophie out of the room. She was at the door when Leroy knocked.

"Come in, hon. Come in and get dry. I sure want to talk to you."

A smile of deep contentment spread across Leroy's face as Fran helped him out of his raincoat, led him into the living room, and immediately nestled closely to him.

"About that divorce, hon—it'll all be over soon. Real soon."

Leroy fumbled hungrily for her breasts, caressing them fiercely, possessively.

"I want you too, darling," she said, kissing him lightly, quickly behind his ear. "But we need privacy. Let's go upstairs."

Fran went behind the curtain and got the upstairs keys from Sophie.

"Here, Leroy, take the key to room six and go upstairs, get undressed, and wait for me. Rush now!"

Almost transfixed with joy, Leroy could hardly move. The rush of her desire for him thrilled him to impassioned heights. Why, why couldn't she be as loving and as close as this all the time?

"Be quiet about it, darling."

In the dim light Fran's eyes seemed to glow, her vibrancy took on an almost electric quality. She guided him to the door and saw him go up the outside staircase. As soon as she came into the warm, dry room, she was sorry for what she had done. It didn't seem so funny any more. But now, even now, was too late. If she turned him back, it would only arouse his curiosity anyway. No, she had made her decision and she had to stick by it.

Sophie rushed out from behind the curtain.

"What's going on here?" she asked, understanding coming horrifiedly into her eyes.

"I gave Leroy the key to Hap Cullen's room and told him to meet me there, that's all."

A shattering scream upstairs drowned the sound of Sophie's astonished gasp.

"The devil himself made you, Fran—not me. You're the meanest bitch I ever knew. You ain't even human. You're a she-devil."

Fran stared stonily at her mother. A quick series of muffled, smashing shocks went on and on in that room upstairs. Thick, heavy cries careened through the air. On and off, a high-pitched, woman's voice shrieked, a violent, tortured Morse code of pain.

Then the sounds of agony ceased. Fran and Sophie moved toward the stairway outside. They walked slowly, as if in a funeral procession, dreading the cruel inevitability they would find in room number six.

The key in his hand, Leroy felt that he held in his fingers the passport to his own Paradise. The fulfillment of his hopes waited behind the door of that room, for Fran would be in that room with him soon ... in his arms and his hair and wrapped in his body so secret and close that she would be part of his heart too.

Excited, he walked along the corridor looking for the room. Before he put the key in the door he noticed a dim light coming from the other side. He laughed to himself—so she had prepared it for him, the cute tease. It made him love her all the more.

And then he had the door open.

In the very first instant he could not accept what his brain commanded him with dreadful clarity to see.

There lay Hap and Edna, bodies still glistening from the warmth of their closeness. They seemed to lie in drowsy depletion, in a slumberous world of their own, that the sound of the door opening abruptly shattered.

Leroy knew one thing, and it buried itself into his consciousness with hideous sharpness. He was the victim of the most dreadful indignity a human being could suffer. This was his own wife locked in the embrace of another man.

A storm of hatred rose up inside him like a hot iron. He lashed out viciously, not primarily against Hap or Edna, but against the accumulated tortures of a destiny that blindly, inexorably was dooming him to a life of bitter tears and savage insult.

He had to move now, to rise up against the confining bonds of the doom that had settled all around him. His hands found a heavy enameled basin and he threw it at Edna. It hit her and she gave a sharp scream, then fell to the floor.

Hap raced toward him and Leroy met him, smashing, slashing, his strength against him in a rage of insane fury. Again and again Leroy drove his fists into Hap's too handsome face. By this time Leroy had lost all control of himself—he was caught in a blind, insensate madness. He saw, as through a red haze, that Hap was still standing and in a sudden surge of ferocity he brought his boot toe up stingingly. Hap's shrill explosion of blinding pain was bloodcurdling. He fell writhing to the floor. And then Leroy fell on him, held his head in his hands as he sat on him, and banged it again and again on the floor.

Leroy didn't know how long he kept pounding. Suddenly his hands seemed heavy, and slippery with a red moistness. Abruptly, he let go the pulpy head of beaten, scarred flesh, almost unrecognizable now.

Whimpering in ceaseless rhythms of despair, Edna huddled in the corner, watching a trickle of blood from Hap's forehead inch toward her. When its warm stickiness touched her cold, quivering flesh she screamed again in toneless horror. Leroy just stood over Hap's body, a creature less than human, now only a hulk whose breath rumbled and strained in heavy agony.

Fran, Sophie and Chunky came through the door together. Fran's face wore a glaze of emotionless calm; only her hands, folding and unfolding over each other endlessly, gave hint of her inner turmoil. Sophie waddled in and began to tremble in terror at sight of Hap's body rigid, rag-limp on the floor. Chunky stood there, somewhat out of it all, with the clear cry of the criminal mind sirening through his brain: see if the body is alive and if it isn't, get rid of it quick!

Unshaven, his suspenders flapping around his waist, Chunky, with his bleary, sleep-fogged eyes, seemed the very picture of slimy, sordid humanity, almost like a natural, putrescent fungus growing out of the very situation he had just intruded himself upon.

"All right, get the girl taken care of!" He motioned toward Edna. Edna came forward gently massaging her smashed nose, trying pitifully to open her bruised and blackened eyes. Then she lay back almost deathlike as Sophie and Fran washed her and calmed her down. Soon her sobs made only a surface static in the noiseless tension of the room.

Leroy slumped now in an armchair, one of Chunky's handkerchiefs wrapped around his battered fists.

"I'll be back," Chunky said.

Soon he returned with a bottle of whiskey and held it to Leroy's lips as one would bottle-feed a helpless child. Leroy sputtered and choked, his chest heaving violently, but his eyes twitched back to life. Chunky clipped him across his face, and soon Leroy's body spasms quieted.

"All right, you two—Leroy and Edna. Get going. Get going now before I call the cops."

Slowly Edna crawled off the bed and came to Leroy. Her hand, extended, searched for his. Together they rose and walked out of the room, out of the house, and into their car. Not once did Leroy look at Hap's bloody body.

When they heard the car pull away, the trio unfroze from their tableau. Chunky went toward Hap's silent body.

"Who is he? Got any folks near here?"

"No one, Chunky. Closest kinfolks are in Arkansas, and they ain't much interested," Fran said, coming to life again as Chunky assumed direction of the brutal course of events.

"Well, he may be dead. Can't tell yet, of course, but it just may be. And I can't have a doctor in here to check. That would mean the cops right behind him." Chunky rubbed his hands over his dirty, whiskered chin. "You go downstairs while I make sure. And, Fran, I'll sure want to see you later. You and me got a lot of business to check over together."

Fran dared not give in to the fright his words provoked in her. She went down with Sophie to the kitchen, made coffee, and sat fearfully waiting for something to happen.

In a few minutes they heard a truck pull up, steps running up and down the outside staircase. The truck used no lights and its great hulk, lit by the street light, loomed in the auto graveyard like the rotting skeleton of a prehistoric machine-monster. Fran shuddered as she watched it, waiting outside the window.

The cops, Fran thought—they would be here soon enough. They would be caught. Hap—was he dead? Could Chunky take care of it? It had all ended so horribly. She hadn't meant it to be this way. All she had wanted was for Leroy to see finally that it was all over.

Turning from the window, Fran caught her mother's eye. Old Sophie was staring at her with undiluted hatred. Fran rose to go to her, but at her first motions toward her, Sophie involuntarily shuddered and moved away from her.

"What am I—a stinking animal?" Fran cried. "I didn't know it would be like this. I didn't know what was going on up there. All I wanted was to get rid of the dumb bastard, that's all."

Sophie shrugged her shoulders, averting her body so that she eluded her daughter's embrace. Together in their dreadful uncertainty, their crushing fear, the two women, now in separate corners of the room, waited out their vigil under the ominous oppression of sure doom.

Hours later Chunky returned. Fran and Sophie sprang from their seats like two tense jacks-in-the-box. Chunky stormed in, looking like death warmed over; his eyes were overcast with a faraway stare of complete self-absorption. When Fran tried to meet his gaze in silent questioning, he avoided her.

Finally Sophie spoke. "Is he—dead?"

"How could any man survive a team of horses stompin' over him? That's what happened to that poor bugger."

"But the body, Chunky. What about the body?"

"It's gone now, Soph. Let's just say that it's gone."

"Where, Chunky, where?" Fran pleaded. "I just gotta know. Maybe I shouldn't, but I gotta know."

"The trucks are loading coal barges down the river. Hap worked at the barges once in a while on a Saturday to make a little extra money. Sometimes a drunken tough falls in a barge and gets himself all twisted up. Nobody cares about river rats anyway."

Fran clutched at her eyes as if to blot out the too graphic picture Chunky had drawn.

"And the truck driver—what about him?"

"Forget it, Fran. Anyway, I'm sure you can forget it. He's done this kind of work before. Now, how about some hot coffee?"

Sophie hastened into the kitchen.

Slowly Chunky moved toward Fran. His eyes now locked in hers, challenging them with a relentlessly cruel gaze. Hate filled them, clouded them, narrowed them to inscrutable depths.

It's like he's measuring me for a coffin he's personally gonna put me in, Fran thought. She turned away from him, but Chunky followed her until he had her in a corner.

He has me now. He thinks he has me now, Fran thought. But it ain't so. He can't do anything about it. Or maybe he can. I don't know which I want more: to get him close to me again—so I can latch on to his dough—or to find a way to keep him off of me.

Sophie returned shortly with steaming cups of dark coffee. Chunky took his gaze from Fran and paid attention to his shoes.

"I was thinkin'," he said softly. "Supposing this hick Leroy starts talking. Maybe he takes Edna to the hospital and the docs start asking questions...then the cops. We gotta take care that they don't answer anyone's questions."

"What do you want me to do?" Fran asked, fearing what he had in mind. Since she had seen Hap's beaten form lying on the floor, the reality of his murder, the enormity of the crime, had slowly sunk in. This was the most horrible crime a human being could be capable of, and though she had not used a weapon on Hap, she was more his murderer than was Leroy.

"Go to him, Fran. Talk to him, persuade him in your own inimitable way." Chunky's voice insinuated a cruelty that frightened Fran anew.

"But what good would it do, Chunky? He's on to me now. Even that big oaf wouldn't fall for anything I'd tell him."

"No, but he'd be sure to appreciate anything you could do for him now, if you know what I mean, old Fran."

Yes, there was still that, Fran thought. But would he want me now? Could desire triumph over the certain distrust he would feel for her. She saw, though, that she had no choice but to make the attempt.

"I'll try it, Chunky, honest I will. Maybe I can get him to go back to the hills, take Edna with him. I'll go up now and get a couple of hours sleep and try first thing in the morning, before he leaves for the plant."

Without saying good night to Chunky or Sophie, Fran left the kitchen and walked toward the stairs. She wanted sleep, to escape into the comforting unreality of dreams. When she entered her room she removed her outer clothes and fell across the bed in her bra and panties. Trying to sleep, she heard the stomping, old man's shuffle of Chunky on the creaking staircase and along the hall. As his steps approached her door, she heard, too, his heavy, grunting breathing. He's like a dirty grizzly bear, she thought, and curled her body under the clean sheets.

In the darkness fear took hold of her as she heard the click-click of the doorknob as it slowly turned. In the half-light of the hallways she saw Chunky standing hesitantly in the threshold.

"What do you want, Chunky?" she almost screamed, sitting up in bed with the coverlet clutched around her bare breasts.

"I want you, you miserable bitch—and tonight I'll have you, too." His voice was a dry rasp of fury.

He advanced toward her, kicking the door shut with his foot. Fran wanted to cry out, but the oppressive insistence of his manner frightened her into silence. Slowly, with calmness, he went about the business of lighting a small lamp. The dimness of the room cast weird shadows on the walls. His form assumed the shape of an unrecognizable monster.

"Go away, you no-good old bastard. You're worthless with a woman, and you know it. Boy, you know it! So don't try to frighten the bejesus out of me."

"Real ungrateful, ain't you, Fran? You don't appreciate what I did with Hap Cullen's body—or anything—including the hundred-dollar bill I'd planned to offer you."

"Look, old goat, you didn't do me any favors. The cops prowling around here wouldn't do you any good either."

All the while he talked, Chunky undressed, slowly, as if he had planned this display of exhibitionism for a long time. He was aware that the sight of his grimy, aged body disgusted Fran, and so each area of flesh he revealed he seemed to thrust before her eyes, now flooded with revulsion. Little details of his person horrified her: the dead whiteness of his sickly skin, the gnarled, twisted hands; the pouchy bags under his eyes, and the eyes themselves, yellowed and bloodshot.

He leaned over her and she recoiled in disgust, and then, in a sudden outburst of panic, she frantically bit his shoulder in an effort to frighten him off.

But now Chunky did not heed her constant insults to the vigor and stamina of his virility. He seemed possessed by a hatred so strong that it powered him with raging energy.

One hand upon her mouth, he forced himself into bed beside her. His other hand caressed the rigid warmth of her entire body. His touch was like waves of ugliness washing over her.

Fran closed her eyes, imagined herself anywhere on earth but here—even in Leroy's arms, even in the brutal Stan's embrace. She tried to lock Chunky's entire being out of her mind, as if by will she could make him disappear. But Chunky's hands continued to caress her; his lips crushed against hers; the weight of his body impressed itself against her.

She felt crushed, consumed in the driving intensity of his revengeful lust. Her abuses rang in the air. Chunky heard only the insatiable call of his passion, now fleetingly triumphant in his body. For everything—the humiliation he had taken from her, the insults, as well as his own needs—he was now taking full revenge.

Fran felt smothered, suffocated, and almost wished she would be.

Her own body lay inert and half-dead. After what seemed to her an eternity, Chunky left her and went to his pockets and extracted a hundred-dollar bill.

"You earned it. You can earn more, too. Plenty more where this came from—and you know it! But you'll only see it a hundred at a time. And now I hope you sleep, 'cause Lord knows, Fran, you won't sleep when you start roasting in hell."

Fran lay sobbing softly. She cursed him, damned him, planned his murder. But words and thoughts were the only revenge she was capable of. Deeper in her mind than these, and more lasting, was the memory of his rape—the rape she had brought upon herself through the stinging pain of her insulting, castrating destruction of his pride.

It was a long while before she was able to sleep, and when she did, she dreamed dreams so awful that in the morning she was grateful for not being able to remember them.

CHAPTER TEN

THE light of the false dawn awakened Fran. For a few minutes she lay in bed, her eyes twitching in a spurt of nervous energy. Her sleep had been fitful, interrupted by dreams of death and vicious abuse at the hands of Chunky. The day itself appeared as an insurmountable challenge. When she remembered her necessary errand—getting Leroy out of town—she fell back against the pillow already exhausted.

In the shower she scrubbed Chunky's soured, unwashed odor from her body. It came to her in a horrible thought that he had left in her the seeds of her own decay, her own destruction; and that those seeds were impossible to root out. Doom, a cloud suffocating and complete, settled upon her like an invisible, ineradicable film.

She dressed quietly, quickly, frightened at the thought of meeting Sophie or Chunky so soon. The streets were deserted, and the absence of people, the silent houses, all created for her the effect that she was abandoned in a world where everyone had died, and that her trip to Leroy was a wandering in hell.

Leroy's house was lighted. He, too, had not slept, Fran thought. Damn him! Why did he ever have to sleep again! Softly she went on the porch and glanced into the living room.

Leroy sat slumped in a chair. His hands were restless, running through his hair, wiping themselves mechanically against the arm of the chair. His eyes were red-rimmed, his hair tousled and his cheeks sunken, haggard and starved-looking. He has seen the devil, Fran thought; perhaps the same one who visited me in *my* awful dreams.

He's dangerous, Fran considered to herself as she stood on the porch, frightened at talking to him again. He's half out of his mind, maybe ready to give himself up to the cops, or lunge out at her. The phrase, "the breaking point," ran through her mind. This was a man at that point. She shivered in recognition of his perilous hold on his sanity.

She did not knock, but instead walked in. Leroy jerked his head up suddenly, his eyes filled with a riot of hurt and pain and naked hatred.

Going to him, she threw her arms about him, sunk her head against his stomach, now tense and defensively muscled. Desperately she realized that her only hope lay in the possibility that he might want her again as a woman, or at least feel protective toward her if he saw her distraught and in open fear.

"Leroy," she said, coaxingly, "believe me. I didn't know— couldn't of known. Now, now I'm here to help you."

"Go home, Fran. You done enough already for me, or to me, whatever the hell it is. Go home!"

He felt her warmth against his rigid body. Her perfumed hair assailed his senses. The memory the body retains for pleasure, for desire, awoke in him. He moaned a little in an effort to hold back his tears and then gave in to despair, to defeat, by holding her tightly in his arms.

Like the scurrying of mice, the shuffling of feet frightened them. Fran turned and noticed Edna standing in the doorway, her face raw, her nose smashed. She said nothing, only stared at Fran, killing her with her hostile detestation.

Suppressing a shudder of self-revulsion, Fran turned from Edna's accusatory gaze and tried again to reach Leroy's shattered senses.

"You've got to get out of town, Leroy," Fran said, impulsively patting his sweat-streaked hair, as though she were calming a helpless little boy. "The cops will be here—no doubt about that. Hap's in the hospital now, very badly hurt. If he should die..."

"Where can I go, Fran? What could I do? I haven't a damn cent to my name now, every penny I have is tied up in those son-ovabitchin' installment plans."

"Leroy, honey, I couldn't stand it if they sent you to prison—and I'll say that right here in front of Edna."

The drama of the moment had completely captivated Fran. She felt now that every word had to achieve an immediately convincing effect in order to save her *own* life. The dingy room assumed the character of a little theatre; she was actress and author of lines that made her now Leroy's judge and jury.

"Go to the hills, Leroy. Your people are there. They'll take care of you. Here's some money. Look! Take care of yourself—for me. I'll let you know the first minute that everything's okay again."

Leroy sat there, weighted down by the accumulated anguish of his whole experience at Power-Trak—the unfriendly city people, the installment plan exploitation, the frustrated lusting after Fran, and now the terrible events with Hap Cullen. A spider web of doom seemed to have caught him, embroiled him. He had to leave it all. If he could only believe in Fran—or himself...

"We gotta go, Leroy. There's no place else we can go to," Edna said, coming to him with her arms extended, anxious to embrace him.

But Fran would not surrender Leroy to his wife. Instead, she held him possessively a moment before releasing him. She turned to leave.

"Write to me, Leroy. Tell me how much you miss me."

The fury on Edna's face, the helpless look in Leroy's sad eyes, all conspired to make Fran almost believe in what she said.

Soon, soon, Fran told herself. Soon she would be far, far away. Damn Leroy and Chunky and Stan and whatever lousy, trouble-making situation they'd try to force her into. In a few days she would have concluded some business "deals", gotten some new hillbillies to buy some furniture on time payment, and collected the last of the old sucker money. Then there was Leroy's house with its new furniture to be repossessed. More money in the bank. The memory of Hap lying in bloody death on the floor was already beginning to fade. Even the degrading hours with Chunky seemed not so bad. In some curious way she could not understand, she took it as due punishment, something she had been deserving for a long time.

But Chunky still had the fortune somewhere. And wherever it was, Fran intended to get at it—by hook or crook or sex-on-the-line, it would be hers. The problem was to make sure that the next time with Chunky would be the last time, the time she'd be sure of knowing where it was.

The weeks passed tensely. True to her word, Fran tried to round out her commitments with the local suckers, but more and more "opportunities" presented themselves. New contracts were awarded to Power-Trak, and that meant that new workers were being imported for the job. It seemed to Fran that half of the hills must be emptying out, the stills abandoned, the pigs left to wallow with the old folks. Like refugees, the hillbillies crowded the roads to Power-Trak—to money, women, and the most expensive cheap furniture they could be sold. And Fran was there to do the selling.

One night, just as she was entering the house, two short, seedy-looking men were leaving. Chunky's friends, no doubt, she thought.

Inside, Chunky sat under the naked light of the living room. His hands gripped a whisky bottle. His eyes were bloodshot and his shoulders sagged in defeat.

"Trouble, Fran old girl," he said, as she stared at him. "One of our 'associates' is doin' a lot of talking. The cops picked up the truck driver who took care of friend Hap Cullen. He was drunk and the cops put him in the overnight tank, but the old boy went blatherin' on—maybe about us. I just don't know."

"Every drunk runs off at the mouth. You know that, Chunky," Fran said, pouring a hard shot of liquor for herself.

"But this fella's been held for four days now. They usually throw 'em out on the street the next day."

"You got money, Chunky. Buy him off, or maybe better yet, buy the cops off. A little dough will spring anybody."

Maybe now, Fran thought, maybe now, with him tired and scared and talky-drunk—maybe now he'll let go with where his money is hidden.

"I don't have that kind of money. You're crazy to think so, Fran. Real crazy to believe an old geezer like me's got bribe-type money."

"You ain't so old, Chunky. You know that. I guess maybe I know that too now."

He grinned at her, lopsidedly, with the spittle dripping, quivering at the side of his lip. Awkwardly he reached for her breasts. Against him now, she pushed strainedly at his shoulders. He tore at her blouse, ripping the front of it more than halfway down. His lips and teeth scraped along her smooth skin. The odor of his body revolted her. She broke away from him and raced toward the door. Angrily, determinedly, he walked toward her. When he came near her, holding the whisky bottle as a weapon, she suddenly reached for it, grabbed it from him and smashed it across his face. He crumpled to the floor, the bottle falling across his chest, spilling its contents in a tiny flood across his heaving body.

Sobbing, she fled to the bathroom. She searched for the light switch and found it. When she turned it on, a little sputter of blue flame burst from it. A tiny spark of electricity pricked her fingertips and she jumped back. This shock and the attempted assault of a few moments ago proved too much for her. Convulsive spasms of fear and depression seized her. She went to the bathroom sink and turned on the cold water full strength. The feel of it cascading over her head and face and back of the neck revived her spirits and her senses.

On top of everything, now there had to be sparks. They frightened her. She had heard of fires starting from something as small as that—of houses being destroyed. Sophie would laugh, maybe, at that, but Fran knew it was true. And thought of a fire breaking out, possibly in the dead of night … She shuddered. She kept seeing visions of the consuming fires of hell.

Well, she thought, she wouldn't be here long, and maybe nothing would happen in that time. On the other hand, maybe …

In the morning, Chunky said nothing; his eyes, however, eloquently testified to his hatred for her. He made no attempt to get back at her. Instead, he announced that he would be out of town for a few days on "business."

That afternoon, Renie and Sophie went to a movie. Fran wondered and worried about the sparks. She thought she'd ask an electrician, who had whistled at her several times in the factory cafeteria, to look into it. He was all too happy to oblige. It was only a few minutes' work to remove the coverplate. On the other side, a small spring clip was soldered to the inside surface. The clip held a small brass key. Fran knew what that was for, and she knew now how to remove the coverplate. The electrician was easy to handle. In a few minutes he went out whistling. Inside of an hour, Fran had the coverplate off again, a duplicate key made, and the coverplate back in place.

The house was quiet now. Sound seemed magnified. The silence itself seemed to rush roaringly around her. In her bedroom she fingered the key as if it were a precious gem. But suddenly the thought sprang up hideously: what good was the key at all to her until she knew to what lock it fitted? Intuitively she had assumed at once that it opened the treasure chest of Chunky's money.

Some time soon, she reasoned, he would have to get more funds. When he did, Fran vowed to herself, she would be behind him, close as his shadow, to seek out his secret. The game was, then, to outwit Chunky, to outwait him. Like a cat stalking the ever-present rat, she would pursue him.

There was a way, she knew, to get him to go to his money. She would wait until he was surely low in funds, then offer herself to him for the usual hundred dollars. Then, warily, cannily, she would learn where the money was hidden.

Her plans made, she spent the rest of the afternoon luxuriating in the advantage of having the house to herself. It was a false freedom, she knew. Soon Stan would be out of the penitentiary; soon Leroy would learn that she had practically railroaded him out of town; soon Chunky would make the fact of his blackmail threat over her head more horribly real.

In almost every way she was doomed, trapped by the greed she had permitted to possess her. But in a way, she determined in that lonely house, that very greed would be her ticket to freedom. She would use every stratagem of cunning to get the money and so happily deport herself away from this increasingly fiery hell on earth.

CHAPTER ELEVEN

THE weeks that followed gripped her as though they were infecting her with a painful disease. Fran grew increasingly irritable; her sense of humor disappeared; her avariciousness grew until all she could think about was money and where to get more of it.

Like a thorn in her side, the key she had taken from the bathroom fixture stabbed at her, taunted her. What did it open? Where? When could she gain access to the fortune Chunky had hidden away?

Most of her waking hours were spent in conniving Chunky into revealing where the money was stored. But Chunky refused to get drunk enough, careless enough, provoked enough. And soon now Stan would be back from the penitentiary.

One night Fran came home in a particularly pained mood. For an hour she had sat with some clumsy oaf of an Arky, being pawed and slobbered over with kisses, being teased and degraded. She had sat patiently stifling her distaste, hoping that he would grow tired and that she could begin to "work" on him, trying to get him to take a new set of furniture for his newly rented house. Only if she would be co-operative, she knew, would he take out the installment plan from her. No permission, no commission—that was the way it was.

When the man's passion had cooled a bit, she gave him her pitch. She was so weary by that time that she didn't even enjoy a sense of triumph when he signed up for a de luxe living room and bedroom suite. She just wanted to be home, away from the dingy, money-grubbing life she had to lead.

And now she was home, and that was not much better. The house stank of stale beer. The rooms were undusted, airless. Supper would again be a pot of stew or some delicatessen food tossed on a greasy plate.

Sophie greeted her with her usual grunt and waved her into the kitchen.

"Letter from your boy friend," Sophie said, stuffing a grimy envelope into Fran's hand.

The back flap had S.W.A.K. scribbled across it in a curiously childish handwriting. A faint aroma of perfume clung to the cheap paper.

"Oh, Lord, Ma, it's from Leroy!"

Fran quickly ripped the letter open. The script was crudely lettered, repetitiously whining and pleading. Fran sneered at the cluster of X's scrawled across the bottom. Then, all at once, the full meaning of what he had written hit her sharply, painfully. Her face whitened and, involuntarily, she gave a short, whistling gasp.

"He wants to—he wants to come back, Ma. Says he's saved up a new stake, and that Edna's more interested in some railroader than in their little baby. Says he's gonna leave her now for good. What the hell does he think I am—his everlovin' soulmate?"

Why now, Fran shouted to herself, why now? Chunky's money was still Chunky's; Stan was gonna be on her tail any day now; she couldn't free herself from the installment buying racket. She was trapped, cornered by her own greed and inability to make a final, decisive move.

"Chunky'll know what to do," Fran said to Sophie as she began to eat the stew set before her.

"I wouldn't bother the old gent right now, Fran," Sophie said, smacking her lips in glee as she slurped the hot stew into her gullet. "He's up there with three colleagues, you might say, talkin' real quiet, even putting a piece of somethin' over the keyhole."

Fran was going to try to get Sophie's goat about being a spy and eavesdropper, but it dawned on her that whenever Chunky took his friends up to his room, money changed hands. Either Chunky was going to make a big deposit or a withdrawal from the horde of cash; one way or the other, she had a chance to follow him to the secret spot.

A swelling tide of expectant excitement flooded through her as she heard heavy steps on the stair. The men soon entered a car, and then Chunky put his key in the door. As he turned the key in the lock, Fran thought of her own key—duplicate of his key—and wondered where she would soon be turning it.

"Good evening ladies, a very good, good evening," Chunky said, almost doing a little jig as he came into the living room.

He sat down next to Fran and ogled her possessively, completely, as if she were a recent acquisition to his harem.

The old goat, Fran fumed, who does he think he is? I'll take some of the sparkle off his smile when I tell him about Leroy coming back.

Sophie brought coffee and the three of them sat in ominous silence, slopping their spoons noisily about.

"I got a letter from Leroy today, Chunky. He wants to come back here to see me."

Fran waited to see the grin disappear, fade into a frightened, vacant stare of disbelief. Instead Chunky almost sang as he whistled over the coffee cup to cool it.

"Fine, have him come with Edna. Be a big reunion here, have a party."

"You're a crazy old coot, Chunky."

"Don't worry any more, Fran. I took care of everything."

She leaned closer to him, gazing at his eyes as if to listen to them, not trusting the casualness of his voice.

"What about Hap, Chunky? And the truck driver. If he talks..."

"That truck driver ain't talking to anybody 'cept Saint Peter, or the devil, dependin'."

"You don't mean—"

Chunky's smile vanished into the icy glare he cast across his face. "The truck driver was pinched again and he went stark staring crazy, crazy as a loon. So crazy he went and hanged himself in his cell. It seems the sergeant just kinda forgot to take away his belt. Of course three hoods from Chicago were in this detention cell with him, having got themselves pinched in a brawl downtown. But the papers won't even mention it."

So this was what the old miser was capable of—murder! Satisfied as she was to achieve a clear-cut solution to her problem, Fran was terrified. If he could do this so coolly, so indifferently, what wouldn't he do to her if he took a real hate against her? Must she fear this man too—aged, half-impotent though he was? Was she always to be at the unreliable mercy of cruel, sadistic men?

"Sorry you couldn't meet the three companions the driver had, but they were rather anxious to go back home to quiet Chicago."

There would be an investigation, Fran knew. Hap had slipped off the surface of the earth, Leroy was gone, now the only witness was murdered. The smallness of her physical presence compared with the vastness of crowds, its ineffectiveness against calculated, destructive evil, filled Fran with a pervasive horror, a dread sense of her own helplessness.

Chunky looked at her slyly, the grin now narrowing as desire flamed into his eyes. And an equally sly look was born in Fran's eyes. This importation of three Chicago toughs took a lot of money. Chunky would have to go to his hiding place soon, very soon, maybe tonight. She would be right there behind him. So large did this plot loom in her thoughts, that she was afraid that Chunky would be able to read her mind.

"So he's dead," Fran went on. "Still, that doesn't make it safe for Leroy to come here, for him or for us."

"Sure it does, Fran. Without the truck driver he couldn't prove a thing. Folks'd think he was a cuckoo; he looks like one when he's roaring angry anyway. Call the cops and run him in, if you want to. I tell you he can't harm us ever."

Probably Chunky had a contact at the police department ready to throw Leroy in the jug and throw the key away if he ever dared to press a complaint or even ask a question. Then one day he would be a "suicide" too.

That problem neatly disposed of, Fran returned to her basic plan of discovering where Chunky had the money. Now she was truly, desperately afraid of Chunky; she knew how far he would go to get whatever he set out to win. But money, the freedom it would buy for her, persuaded her that any risk was worth taking, because any fate she would meet at the hands of Stan, or the possible cruelty of one of her hillbilly clients, would be a kind of death in itself.

"Guess you're gonna celebrate, right, Chunky?" Fran leaned closer to him, letting him draw in her perfume with his breath, letting the silk of her blouse rustle against his shoulder.

"I'd sure like to," Chunky answered, lowering his eyes, a small smirk forming at the corners of his lips.

"Well, I'll be going up to take a bath, Ma," Fran said, stretching as she rose from the couch. Her hips rolled tauntingly as she walked slowly out of the room.

She went upstairs, put on a filmy, translucent nightgown, dashed some more perfume on, powdered, put on the full production routine. Then she came downstairs, sauntering into the living room as if she were modelling the nightgown.

"I—I forgot the cigarettes."

"Lord, Fran, put something on. Chunky here—"

"Aw, he's an old friend of the family."

She stressed the world 'old' ever so slightly, trying to rouse Chunky into aggressive action. She leaned against the doorjamb waiting for the cigarettes to be brought to her by Sophie. She leaned forward slightly, and the top half of the gown fell aside, exposing her breasts down to the curve. The nipples appeared as dark target points upon which Chunky fixed a steady gaze. A bit of spittle began to form at the sides of his lips.

"Here's your cigarettes, Fran—now git," Sophie said, and then she grew huffy and turned her back on Fran.

It was just the opportunity Fran had been waiting for. In the instant Sophie's back was turned, she intercepted Chunky's stare and motioned him upstairs with a vigorous toss of her head. Almost imperceptibly, Chunky answered her, nodding agreement to her invitation.

Sophie had gone to sleep early. Fran took her bath and did not stay upstairs, though she knew that Chunky had gone to his room. She waited, now fully dressed, in the living room, waited until Chunky's agony of lustful expectation would reach a crescendo. A gnawing doubt that he would not have to go for his money took hold of her. It seemed to shrivel her; she fought it as one would fight the onslaught of a fatal fever. He must need money; she'd make him need the money, raise her price if necessary. Do anything if necessary. There was not much time.

A little after midnight she went upstairs. The light was on in Chunky's room. He expected to be rewarded for taking care of the truck driver. The glimmer of light seemed unnaturally bright in the pitch-black hallway.

Fran passed his room and went into her own. She undressed and got into bed, shivering as her naked body slid in between the sheets. The alarm clock ticked on. Then a slight scratching sound began; it was Chunky at the door. She knew it, and both feared and was glad of it.

She unlatched the door almost in the same motion she used in getting out of bed, but she did not unchain it. Her manner was cautious, almost surprised. Her perfume choked the musty night air.

"Open up, dammit," Chunky rasped.

"The money. Did you bring the money with you? The hundred?"

"You'll get it. Come on!"

He slipped his hand through the door and it brushed against her thigh. It startled her. She almost slammed the door against his hand.

"Cut that crap, Chunky."

"I'll get the hundred first thing in the morning. I promise."

"No good, Chunky boy. Get the dough now. And my price is now two hundred. You seemed to like it so much, I thought that the traffic could take it."

"Why, you—"

"Don't forget, I'll be sober this time. It won't be like making love to a boozy corpse."

"In the morning, I'll—"

"No rush about it. I'm tired now anyway."

She knew she had him. He was hooked, hooked as sure as any dope addict. It was because he was old; it meant more to him. He had to prove that he was still good—she knew that; he did too. And for him each time was like the last time—maybe. He always had to try again, and nothing, no insult or trickery, could deter him. Pride and hatred and lust commingled and compelled him on.

"I'll be back," he said. "I'll be right back. Stay right here." His footsteps disappeared.

I'll know now, Fran said to herself. I'll be there right behind you, you old coot. And in the morning I'll be on the first plane out of here. No, that'll be too soon. But any day.

She dressed quickly, completely. If she guessed correctly, he'd be making a hurried trip outside. Fully alert, ready for anything, she sat in a chair near the living room door, straining to hear the slightest sound.

As she waited, waves of fatigue assailed her, followed by periods of nervous exultation. She was living now on a plane of almost unreal tension. If something didn't give soon, she would crack, crack like a thin reed snapped by a brutal fist. The silence was such that she could hear the house "breathe," hear the trees shudder in the wind.

Upstairs a key turned. Chunky was coming out of his room. She heard him stop at her door and listen for a moment. Then the footsteps again. The door to the back stairs opened. His steps creaked on them.

Through the window she saw him enter the auto graveyard. His black shape loomed like a corpse awake. Stealthily she followed him. He stopped before a wreck of a car, half hidden by two others that served as barriers to it. He bent over the wrecked trunk of this car and worked a key into it.

It was all she wanted to know. Quickly she ran back to the house and got into bed. Her mind already planned how she would open that trunk and take everything in sight. Soon she was almost half asleep, dreaming of lolling on the beaches of Hawaii.

Again there was the scraping at the door. Chunky had returned with the two hundred dollars. "You know what you can do with it!" Fran hissed. Drawing the blanket over her ears, she burrowed deeply into the pillow, and heard only the waves lapping against the sundrenched shore of Wakiki.

Somehow during the next few weeks she avoided meeting Chunky. Fran quit her job, withdrew her savings, terminated her deals with furniture jobbers and wholesalers. A fully packed suitcase stood in the dark recesses of her closet. As soon as she succeeded in cleaning out Chunky's cache, she would fly to the coast. For hours she used to sit fingering the thin brass key, yearning for that one great chance to use it.

Night after night went by but Chunky did not leave the house. He seemed always to hover around Fran, insulting her with his looks, reaching for any part of her body that came within his grasp. Many times she was tempted to turn her back on caution and make a daring move to get the money, but she knew that she would never have two chances, and that if she would fail, she would be completely at the mercy of Chunky's revengeful heart.

Time and time again she watched Chunky make his trips into the auto graveyard. She was annoyed that he came back with little paper bags full of money. It had almost begun to seem to her that he was now a trespasser on *her* horde of money. Resentment grew in her like a cancerous growth; it threatened to drive her mad.

The weather was turning warm and Chunky resumed his habit of taking a walk for an hour or two after supper. One evening Fran had been standing in the kitchen when a page from the calendar came off the wall and brushed against her apron. On it was a notation: "Stan back any day." Then she knew that she had to act quickly—that night, in fact.

Fran wondered where he went on those walks. Not to the auto graveyard, she was sure. Where then? Probably over to a cheap bar and grill about ten blocks away run by a friend of his from the old country.

If she could make the break during the course of one of these evening walks, Fran calculated, she could be on a plane before he would discover the robbery.

A mist began to fall, a tempting, almost perfumed mood hung over the city. Spring meant renewal, and even old, super-cautious Chunky couldn't resist taking a walk on a lilting night like that.

A dark coat drawn over her traveling clothes (she was set to go at a moment's notice), she followed Chunky until he passed the street light at the next corner. She wanted to make sure that he would not suddenly turn back. When she was convinced that he was heading toward the bar, she turned on her heels and headed for the auto graveyard.

A catlike tension spread in her. She felt almost weightless, and could hear the blood pounding in her ear as she approached the car.

The graveyard was dark, no sound but the night noises, quiet, listening noises, disturbed her theft. The key turned easily, the trunk opened swiftly. She flashed a tiny match flame inside. Nothing was in there except an old inner tube.

It couldn't be. No. Not after all this waiting and planning and the tension like a sickness in her stomach.

The warped floorboards caught her eye. The edges were rotted. Without real hope, she pried one or two up with the key. They gave easily. She lit another match and flashed it again into the space they made.

Neat rows of currency, row upon row, like bricks in the foundation of a building, faced her. More packages, squat, plump, filled another section in the false bottom of the trunk. One squeeze of a few of them convinced Fran that they were jewels.

Hysteria, the wildest kind of relief, almost swept away her senses. Her fingers shook so violently that she dropped the bundle of money she held.

As she reached down to pick it up, she noticed the light flashing on in Chunky's room.

She wanted to scream, to curse, to kill, but as she saw the light go out and his shape come down the outside stairs and toward the auto graveyard, she sprang into action automatically. Working feverishly, the sweat streaking her face like dried tears, she returned the board and put back the false bottom of the trunk.

As soon as she was finished, she noticed Chunky at the entrance to the auto graveyard. She dodged behind some other old cars to watch him. He stood for a moment as if surveying the scene and then he walked back to his room.

Fran was utterly unnerved now. She dared not try it again that night. As she walked, however, her step grew lighter and lighter; it was almost as if she walked on air. Soon she broke into a kind of run. She did not go any place in particular; she just moved, moved, moved away from that horrible auto graveyard.

When she could walk no more, she took a late bus back to her house. It was dark, completely dark, as if abandoned. She climbed the stairs slowly, thinking of when she could try again. It would have to be a time when the entire house was empty; her heart couldn't take another shock like that.

Sleep, she thought; she needed sleep. Tonight she would let herself lose all consciousness. She wouldn't wait to watch Chunky's moves. In the morning she would plan again.

Quietly she put the key in the door. She didn't turn on the light. She didn't think she could stand any sharp brightness. Mechanically she stripped her clothes from her body. Fatigue had conquered. She slipped into bed, and her heart seemed to freeze.

The scream she gave was muffled against a heavy, hard-skinned hand. Suddenly the overhead light went on, almost blinding her. Her wildly frightened eyes knew at once then.

In the bed, next to her trembling body, was her husband Stan. On the floor, strewn roughly across the room, lay the contents from her suitcase.

The expression on his face was not one of love, or even desire. It was pure, unmerciful hatred.

"You bitch, you miserable, greedy bitch!"

Stan released his hand from her mouth. He looked down at her, supported by one elbow, watching terror creep into her eyes.

"But you aren't supposed to be here yet, Stan."

In her fright only the brutal truth escaped Fran's lips. Her body shuddered as he passed his hand over her breasts, her stomach, probed the softness of her thighs.

"I see you've been doin' all right for yourself, Fran. Your bankbook makes interesting reading. You're gonna be a source of comfort and security to me in my old age."

"It was all for us, to go away together. I swear it."

Fran would have sworn to anything. She knew what to expect—a vicious beating, maybe even disfigurement. No fine point of cruelty and degradation escaped Stan when the fury was upon him.

"Not even a five-dollar bill all that time I was in stir. Weeks went by without even money for a cigarette."

Fran's body seemed to dissolve, to shrink. Fear paralyzed her, numbed her brain.

"Where did that bank balance come from? Come on, talk—or do you want me to loosen your tongue in my own inimitable way?"

He leaned the weight of his heavy, naked body upon her own. His face came toward her, then turned. For a brief second she thought he wanted to kiss her. But instead he caught the lobe of her ear in his teeth and bit hard. She screamed once, sharply.

"Just a love tap, darling. Now, where did that money come from?"

"Wait, Stan. Listen. I worked and saved up until I had enough to get you a new trial, or maybe just to make things easy for us when you did get out. Then the lawyers said that no new trial was possible. So I just saved and saved."

"On that dinky salary Power-Trak paid you? Who are you kidding?"

"Honest, Stan … "

"You don't know what the word honest means."

Fran cowered. She was unable to move. A light cold sweat covered her body.

"Come here, don't crawl away from me."

This was my husband, Fran thought. Still is, I suppose, but he's no more than a dangerous stranger to me now. And yet he's still good-looking, still the sexiest man I ever knew. Prison has only made his body leaner, more muscular than ever. But she didn't desire him; she was revolted by the power he had over her. The question was, how to escape. Somehow she had to get away from him.

"You're my wife, remember? I've been in prison a good long time now without a woman. You know what it's like? It's like living on bread and water all the time remembering what a full steak dinner is like."

His hands seized, it seemed, all the parts of her body at once. The kisses he gave her were sharp, searing touches of a flame. At first she was aware only of his heaviness, the hard touch of his hand. Then, the way he knew how to so well, he began to waken the dead desire she had once had for him. Soon her body did not obey her brain, which told her to thrust his presence away. Her arms encircled his broad back, her fingers felt the strain of his throbbing muscles. And then her limbs melted at his touch.

There was no pleasure and there was no pain for her, only a limitless awareness of being alive in every tiny secret corner of her body. And when he was quiet and spent, master of her once again, the fervor and abandon she surrendered to him did not die with his satiation. Tremors of anguished need coursed through her body. Shamelessly, against every sane thought her mind could create for her to see, she wanted him again. And she knew, finally, that she would desire him always.

"You're still a damned good lay, Fran. Always was, always will be. You take a lot out of a man, but it's pleasure well spent."

He began to breathe more slowly. Soon he would descend into a languor, then a heavy, deathlike sleep. Like a great animal, he slept contented after taking her.

If she could arouse him soon, then surely he would exhaust himself, sleep. But she was fooled. Stan lay back, drowsily smoking a cigarette. She touched him, but he turned away. Clearly, he was in no more mood for sex.

He sat up in bed. She glanced at him in despair. There could be no escape tonight. The sex had only reinvigorated him.

"There's six grand in that suitcase. What did you hang around for—the full sixty-four thousand dollars?"

At these words a scheme took shape in Fran's mind. She had learned her lesson; she had been too greedy. Perhaps now she could escape with her own saved money at the cost of sacrificing Chunky's cache to Stan. Surely the safety of her own life made it worth the try.

"Call that real money?" she said. "Hell, I know a haul cased that'll make six grand look like small change."

A malicious delight filled her as she saw the disbelief and cunning shadow Stan's eyes.

"What kind of phony crap you handin' me?"

"It's true—I swear. You know Chunky, that old miser who's lived here for years and years. Well, he's got a hoard of money big enough to finance a foreign loan."

"So?"

"So I know where the money is. I was going to clean it out tonight. That's why I was all set to clear out."

"What's it all about?"

She told him where the money was hidden, less than a hundred feet from where they spoke. And told him, too, that Chunky was far away, getting looped in a bar. All through the description of how to get the treasure, Stan said nothing. Occasionally his eyes searched hers, giving her a kind of X-ray glance in an attempt to guess the truth or falsehood of her statement.

"C'mon, let's get dressed," he said when she had finished.

"You mean—?"

"Right. We take the old coot's cash together, and then lam out of here fast as an airplane can carry us. Right to—well, wherever the first plane out of here is going."

They dressed and he motioned for Fran to lead the way. She walked slowly, hoping that Chunky had heard them. Usually nothing escaped his prying ears and eyes. Let him catch Stan, she hoped. She took no precautions at all against the noise of their movements.

Stan's belief in her was reinforced when, in the auto graveyard, she gave him the brass key. He fumbled clumsily as he felt about in the darkness for the keyhole, haste and greed combining to make his fingers awkward. Utterly absorbed in getting the lid open, he did not notice Fran removing the little flashlight from her purse.

Quickly she held it toward the house and flashed it on and off, on and off. If Chunky were watching at all, this sudden bursting on and off of light near his money would surely send him running. Maybe he would be armed, Fran hoped, and would kill Stan on the spot. At least Stan would be returned to prison for attempted theft.

At last her prayers were answered. Heavy, scuffling footsteps crunched over the cinders. Stan continued to stuff the wads of money into Fran's big paper shopping bag. Stealthily, Fran slipped off into the shadowy darkness. Almost by instinct she worked her way around the abandoned autos until she was back at the house. All she heard was the heavy banging of the car trunk and the thuds and smacks of colliding bodies. Grunts and curses filled the air. There was one long wheeze that turned into a short, sharp scream before silence devoured it. Calmly, rather joyfully almost, she waited for a pistol shot. One good bullet right to the heart could settle all her problems, she decided. It was as simple as that. Only not quite, for it seemed that neither Chunky nor Stan had brought a gun.

She was in the room, a dim light burning, when Stan stormed in. The contents of Chunky's trunk was stuffed in a pillowcase and a paper bag. He reached into her valise and took the six thousand dollars and stuffed it into the pillowcase.

"Be seeing you, dear wife and lover," he said sneeringly. "Have my mail sent to the Y. If I can sneak in again, like I sneaked out to come here, I'll have the perfect alibi."

"Stan, you didn't—"

"I had to. He went off his nut when he saw me and came at me like a lion. I conked him with an old car axle. It smashed his head like an egg. Nobody saw me, nobody. I'll get away with it. Or—"

He turned to her, a heavy porcelain wash basin in his hand. Slowly he came toward her, brandishing it like a sword.

"No, Stan. I won't tell a soul. I swear."

She blurted the words out in a quick, fearful jumble. Fright was making a defenseless, crawling creature of her.

"Okay. I'll believe you for as long as it's safe to believe you. If I hear you squawked, you'll get it sure as he did."

He rummaged inside the pillowcase and took out her money again, tossing it to her contemptuously.

"Take the cash and keep quiet till this blows over. I'll be back soon as I can and we'll split the rest. In my own way, you know, I'm real sweet on you. As I said, you're the best lay in town, if you're nothin' else."

The amazing drive for self-preservation forced her to swallow her pride in the face of his stinging words. She even managed to respond to his hurried kiss.

"Take care of yourself, Stan. I'll be here—be here for you."

When he went out the door, she collapsed to the floor sobbing uncontrollably.

CHAPTER TWELVE

L EROY walked the streets of the city confused, lost in his disil-lusionment, wretched, almost physically ill with longing for Fran.

One night the despair of his situation crept up on him and horrified him with the hopeless picture it presented. Edna and he were living in a cell-like room in a small Southern city. Clothes were tossed everywhere about the room. In the air was the odor of the baby's neglect—sour milk, the perpetual smell of urine. In the midst of it all sat Edna, bloated, double-chinned, munching on the eternal chocolate candy bar. The baby cried, cried again, but Edna did not move. Instead, she mentioned that it was time to do her nails again, and would Leroy be a good boy and run down the block and get her a bottle of Red Riot color.

Leroy was anxious to leave the dingy apartment. He went to the bureau to look for some change. When he opened the drawer he knocked aside a pile of folded handkerchiefs and exposed a packet of contraceptives. They were not his brand. In the dark he would never have known, but now the evidence against Edna was unmistakable. A woman never bought these things. A man must have been here and put aside some for the next time. Well he would have plenty of next times—all the times in the world, because Leroy had had enough!

Edna greeted his announcement of hatred and intention of departure with cold indifference. She had become pregnant again, she said, and it could be Leroy's kid or the other man's; she didn't know and didn't much care. There would always be a man for her, to take care of her.

Leroy threw some underwear, ties and a shirt and pair of trousers into an old dufflebag and cleaned out the bureau drawer of most of the money. When he went out the door there were no goodbyes or even expressions of hatred. The deadness in the air was eloquent testimony to the degeneration of their relationship. He took the night bus to the world of Power-Trak, and boarding it, he felt that he had left a kind of prison world behind him. Ahead lay freedom and Fran, which were one and the same thing.

He arrived in the city and immediately went to the factory. First he found out that Fran had quit some time ago. Then he signed on for the same job he had before. The rest of the day was his, and his first stop was Fran's house. Sophie had nothing to say to him, but as he went toward the bus, Renie stopped him and told him that Fran had hit the big time with her husband.

"Look for a big pink Cadillac parked outside of the fanciest club in town—that's them!" she said, and her eyes glittered with envy.

And now he wandered from one club to another. The evening covered the squalid decay of the city. The whole world seemed to Leroy to be run-down, dilapidated. Everybody seemed to be racing along on a treadmill. Suddenly Leroy felt tense, nauseous all over. He had to turn away, or become sick. His feet seemed to slide over the city pavements, so fast did he run from that rat race.

Coming around one of the streets in the theatre district, he saw it. He could not miss it. The gaudy car sat at the curb like a huge, exotic fruit dropped from an invisible palm tree. It glittered and shimmered in the night light.

The swank club it was parked in front of awed Leroy. The windows were covered with elegant brocade hangings. The lettering was small, old-fashioned script. No jazzy neons to lure the suckers, he thought. Maybe 'cause no suckers would go into a swell joint like this.

A doorman, got up in a luxurious arrangement of gold braid and military overcoat, lounged just inside smoking a cigarette. When he was finished he stepped outside and immediately seemed to grow four inches in stature. His shoulders were thrown back, his head struck a noble pose. All in all, he dazzled and frightened Leroy with his studied magnificence.

Leroy would never have dared to go in had not someone come by to talk to the doorman. Quickly, stiff-legged, Leroy dashed past him down the few steps into the club. He was surprised that the doorman did not follow him down and throw him out.

The room he entered was a dimly lighted low-ceilinged retreat. Tinkly music filtered through its smoke-filled air. The women all wore dark, rich colors and fabrics, and their shoulders were all bare and a little glistening under the glare of the brighter lights at the bar. The men were soft-spoken, self-possessed, confident in their wealth and power. But it was all at once just a bar to Leroy. Fancier, quieter, a nicer class of "clientele," but still just a place where men and women met, drank, and made a date to make love together a little later on in the evening. Something like a measure of sureness came to Leroy.

He stood at the entrance to the room surveying the crowd with a steady gaze, ignoring the attempted interference by some of the waiters.

There was an empty stool at the bar and he went to it. Sitting down, he ordered a bourbon and soda and turned his back on the bartender, again staring at the crowd, hoping to see Fran before she saw him.

Slowly he became aware of the conversation behind him. The bartender was talking to a flashily dressed, aging man to the right of Leroy. It was the same old talk, only now the speakers were better educated, more wealthy; but still just as violently bigoted.

"Sure, he may look like something the cat dragged in," the customer said to the bartender, "but its cats like that that buy my eighty-dollar suits, marked up for special resale from forty-five dollars."

"Maybe for you it's okay. Not for me. A class joint doesn't stand a chance around here. All these hillbilly folk want is a twenty-five cent glass of rotgut. They're ruining every decent neighborhood in town. Hell, this place is getting to look more like Turkey Track, Arkansas, than Turkey Track itself."

Leroy was just about to quit the place when he spied Fran. At the far end of the room was a little, but very elegant staircase. Centered at the top of it was Fran, her red hair cut very short, all dressed up in a tight green gown that was made of the plushiest velvet he had ever seen. A mink stole was carelessly slung over one shoulder. Across her exposed chest glittered a wide collar of diamonds.

For a second Leroy didn't recognize her, but then she leaned forward, her cleavage coming provocatively into view. And then he remembered the times he buried his face upon her breasts, and he was sure as his knowing flesh that it was his Fran.

Seeing her at last did not move him as much as he had feared and hoped it would. The splendor of her costume told him more powerfully than any words of the barrier that had sprung up between them.

Something in the deepest part of his heart seemed to speak to him, to warn him that he should forget ever meeting her again. She began to walk down the staircase toward a group of laughing people waiting for her, and he thought of a short, but murderous green snake slithering along a golden desert.

And yet he went forward to meet her, driven by the same nameless compulsion that had made him crawl and cringe and degrade himself for her time and time again. He could not understand his need for her, had no words to give to it. He felt it, felt it as compelling within him as he was sure drunks found compelling the endless urge to hit another bottle for just one more time.

"See you at the Pharoah Club," Fran said to a dark-haired young woman who was heading toward the checkroom.

Lost in the midst of the crowd, Fran did not notice Leroy at all, nor even the cab he trailed her in, all along the way to the club.

It was a long ride, an expensive one for Leroy, but like the hunter who at last has sighted the spoor of his prey, he could not give up. The cab scooted across a river that separated the industrial core of the city from the outlying suburbs. It took a back road and followed it for more than a mile. In the still of the wooded darkness Leroy thought he could hear shouts of laughter and drunken cries from the crowded car in which Fran sat.

Music floated through the air. It seemed to come from a great distance, then suddenly grew louder. Leroy realized that some-one had turned up the volume on a radio or phonograph, for soon Fran's car had stopped. His own pulled up alongside, but he waited, hidden in the back of the car, until Fran and her party went inside.

He got out and stood uncertainly, hands in his pockets, listening for a moment to the sound of his taxi rumbling away. The stars seemed to descend on him. The night was an infinite crown of jewels.

Thirty or forty feet away stood a building that looked abandoned, or at least condemned. Faintly he heard the relentless sound of water hitting a shoreline. He must be near Staunton Lake, and this was Staunton Lodge, once a summer estate, now reputed to be a high-class gambling casino—with rooms for "special parties" upstairs.

Lights peeped discreetly from almost completely shuttered windows. From his spot they looked like fireflies winking at him, luring him on.

No one questioned him when he entered. The person who admitted him must have assumed that he was invited along with the rest, and that his poor clothes were a personal eccentricity. He sat at the bar and ordered a bottle of beer.

In the huge mirror over the bar, Leroy noticed Fran rise drunkenly to her feet, propose a toast, and, before she could finish her speech, fall back helplessly to her seat.

Again Leroy was assailed by a vague feeling of indifference, as though he were not so emotionally involved, but were actually a stranger to the entire scene. And yet he could not turn and go. The urge to chance further humiliation dragged him on to this endless slavery to a woman who clearly despised him.

A hard-faced, sullen-lipped man stood behind Fran's chair. As he spoke his hands caressed her naked shoulders lazily, as if he petted a dog or the satiny wood of an expensive piece of furniture.

If this was the hated Stan, Fran gave no obvious sign that she was captive of his brutality. She glowed when he bent down and kissed her quickly on her ear.

Leroy lost himself in a fantasy in which he was Stan's body, kissing Fran, surrounding her with luxury. But then reality returned like an engulfing shadow, and Leroy's thoughts turned to the practical question of when and how he would get to be alone with Fran.

Almost in answer to his silent wish, someone came to whisper a message in Stan's ear, and the man left Fran and went into an adjoining room.

Like a swimmer bracing his legs for a kickoff, Leroy placed both hands heavily on the bar and jumped off the stool. This was the first bit of good luck he had had since his search for Fran began. He felt a little light-headed, not in happiness but in fear, at the mere thought of being so close to her. His slow, slightly unsteady walk toward her, was like a march of a penitent. No desire filled his body, only a sense of shame and hurt. He could feel her rejection before she even glanced at him, and perversely welcomed it like a cooling sip of delicious poison.

"Well, my old friend, lover and valued customer, Mr. Leroy Landers!" cried Fran as she first saw him coming toward her.

The room turned as one face to stare at him in his weakness.

"What brings you back, old satisfied customer, another one of Fran's guaranteed genuine bargains? I hate to tell you, you happy hick, but I closed up shop long ago, soon as my man Stan came back from his long stay at the State monastery."

The crowd laughed raucously.

Leroy heard them, but went on, now a bit more steadily, until he stood in front of Fran. His silence cowed Fran's throng of admirers. They backed away, leaving Fran and Leroy alone at the table.

"Got a bargain for you, old Leroy. Another sterling item from my dear old daddy's hope chest."

"Fran, let's go. Let's get out of here," Leroy said sternly.

"It's a pleasure-giving device you'll need if you're still passing away these long evenings with that slob of a wife of yours." Fran gave no attention at all to Leroy's urgent plea.

"What about that divorce, Fran? What about the beatings Stan used to give you? Ain't nothing true about you? You promised to wait till I came back."

"Wait for you? I'm gonna get me any man I want, and Stan won't lay a hand on me again. I got too much on him for him to try any stuff like that."

"I believed in you, Fran. I really did. I—"

His sincerity calmed the sneer in Fran's voice just a bit.

"Look, you goof. Go back home to Arkansas. The cops'll be on your tail pretty soon."

Leroy rose in a vain attempt to be dignified and hurt.

"You killed Hap, Leroy. You know that. The cops know it too. Now go back to those hills and don't crawl out, not even for groundhog day."

Leroy looked with horror at her. His mouth hung slackly while his brain struggled to comprehend the danger inherent in her words of warning. It was another lie of hers, he said to himself. But, staring into her intense, set face, he knew it wasn't.

"It's all over between us, Leroy. You just better see that. You got a little somethin' for your money's worth, a helluva lot more lovin' than most."

"I can't go away, Fran. I left Edna to stay here with you. I love you."

He reached for her, grabbed at her elbow, at her gloved hand. The eye of his mind instantly gave him an image of himself as he appeared to the crowd around them—a shabby, degraded, beaten man, crawling for a kind word from a heartless bitch.

Fran pushed him aside easily and laughed along with the rest of the gamblers. All Leroy now wanted to do was to somehow leave that room and drag his tail out into the night. He tried to rise to go, but could only twist around half-upright in his chair. As he turned he glanced up and felt the intense hatred in Stan's bitter stare.

"This rube's getting wise, Stan. Boot him out!"

Fran's voice had a nervous, hysterical edge to it that she could not completely control.

He was alone now, Leroy thought to himself, all alone in a den of lions, a gambling den of lions. He sought help from Fran and found only contempt, utter rejection. And then he knew, knew at last, and perhaps too late, all the evil that she harbored in her lovely body.

His tongue began to make an effort to speak, to explain to Stan the exact situation, but fear tripped his words, the defeat he had suffered robbed him of any strength of purpose. He felt at the mercy of a hostile rival. If only Stan would make his move, anything to set him free from the awful uncertainty and shame of his humiliated position. Stan's friends gathered about him, forming a menacing circle around Leroy. The club owner sent his bouncer.

"A pleasure," the burly man said. His eyebrows were thick, straggly. He looked as if his hair and eyebrows were one expanse of wild growth.

The orchestra resumed playing. A half-dozen couples were urged out on the dance floor. Gradually the club reacquired its festive air.

Stan ignored the bouncer and instead slowly reached for his gun holster, hidden under his left armpit. Fran saw him and quickly threw her arms about him, covering his hard, lined face with sharp, briefly passionate kisses to dissuade him from shooting.

"Let's dance," she said, leading him to the center of the floor. Over her shoulder she noticed the waiters and the bouncer helping Leroy to his feet. They dragged him out of the club.

The rush of night air reinvigorated Leroy. The agony of his wobbly exit from the club soon faded under the coolness of the outside. Under a thin but bright moon he made his way along the edge of the cindered parking lot, neither looking ahead or back; but only on the ground.

As he walked, kicking the debris of tin cans and broken glass, it seemed that he walked amid the wreck of his own life. He was kicking over the traces as he walked away from Fran and the club and the last illusions he would ever have about their "love" together.

There was no thought of tomorrow or next week or next month. His thoughts centered about his return to his dingy room. It seemed like paradise to him now, a safe retreat away from the degradation he had endured for so long.

And then he heard them, the footsteps racing toward him in that lonely night. They were the steps of a man unaccustomed to running. When they came a bit closer he could hear a slight wheezing.

So he couldn't even crawl back to his room and die a little, Leroy thought. Dismay, fear of certain collapse in the face of this new pressure, erupted in him. He could run to the highway and cut off along the marshes, but he knew he couldn't run forever.

Hands in his pockets, he stood rigid, his body trembling, in the middle of the empty lane. He was terribly afraid. It was as simple as that. More than anything, he wanted to race out of there.

The runner was almost upon him now. So he waited for his fate to show itself.

In his arms, dancing close to him, Fran was aware of Stan's restless ferocity. The gentle rhythms of the slow fox trot only accentuated the burning tenseness in his body. She was sober now, but she could sense his pent-up anger making him drunk in a vicious, kill-for-kill's-sake kind of a way.

"Damn him, Fran!" he said, spitting out the words like little explosions of acidlike hatred, "I'm gonna murder that hillbilly bastard!"

"Forget it, Stan. He's just a punk."

"They're all like that. Those rubes think they own us nowadays, think they can get away with anything."

"The bouncers'll take care of the creep. Don't you worry! And don't you go messing in, 'cause you know how the cops treat ex-cons who get in trouble."

"To hell with the cops! Somebody's got to do somethin'. The hill rats buy a bottle of beer and they think that makes 'em buddies to us all."

The words poured quickly out of his mouth. He seemed to hiss, his voice grew clipped and sharp. It was boiling out of him, Fran could see, boiling out like steam simmers out of a teakettle until the lid flew off. If she could only keep him here another couple of minutes, until Leroy had a good head start the hell out of this place.

Stan kept turning to the door. His grip on her loosened. She would apply a little sure-fire psychology.

"Hon, I'm kinda ready for bed. Not tired, mind you. Just—er—*ready* for bed. How about you?"

"Hell, I'm always ready. You know that."

"Then let's go, lover."

"No, not yet. You go fix yourself up, and I'll get another drink. I don't want to jump into bed with you, mad at the whole world."

His smile convinced her. She glided out of his arms and went to the powder room. Just as she got to the door, she turned around to give him a farewell glance, but it was too late.

"Stop him! Stop him!" she cried out to someone, anyone. "He's got a gun. Don't let him out!"

The bouncers didn't move. She ran toward Stan, but he was already a shadow in the night. Dragging her feet, she returned to the crowd.

"Don't worry now, he'll cool off," the manager said, rubbing his hands across her bare shoulders just a little too caressingly for pure sentiment. "They always cool off."

"Not him, not him. He just goes up in flames. He never cools off."

The crowd of women around her laughed immoderately. They took it as a dirty joke. In a way it was. Fran covered her face in her folded arms as they rested on the table. It was a posture of self-protection, and she needed it; her world was shattering about her.

As if set to come in on cue as grim background music to this emotional disaster, two shots rang out, then a third.

Fran shuddered convulsively, but there were no more tears. Only the dead memories of all her ruined wishes.

In a way each of us sort of looks for his own death; it just doesn't come up at him, Leroy thought as he stood rooted to the ground in the darkness, waiting for the unknown runner, messenger of his death, to approach him. I could go now, but I don't. Something doesn't let me. Why? All Leroy knew was that he was tired, tired finally of running away from his life, tired of running into more and more trouble of one kind or another. This would be his last stand, or maybe the beginning of a new, determined, self-reliant existence. But he would wait it out and see.

A white blur, seemingly disembodied and almost phosphorescent in the star glow, came bobbing into view. A furious desperation seized him. Was this not the phantom death? he thought.

And then the features showed themselves. Not just a nose, a mouth, eyes, a set chin; but a concentrated assault of unparalleled malice—Stan's face, the devil-face Fran had made love to.

Fifteen feet away from him Stan halted. His breath vied with the wind to make himself heard.

"I got a gun, you hillbilly bastard. And I'm gonna use it."

Leroy lunged toward him half-running, half-leaping. His aim was to reach Stan before he loosed the bullet. But Stan raised the gun like a bludgeon, and Leroy felt the crack of it over the back of his neck. His punishment was a pistol whipping—at least for a start.

Again the gun butt hit him, this time high on the cheek. The bone was exposed, then the raw and bleeding flesh. Impervious to anything but the searing, overpowering rain of pain throughout his body, Leroy plunged in again.

Unseeing, his body grappled with Stan's. He managed to grasp Stan's wrist and he twisted the muzzle of the gun away from himself. Enraged, he threw his entire weight against Stan's chest and shoulders. Stan struggled with fanatic fury, but his luxury-loving body was no match for Leroy once it was girdled by the farm man's iron-banded muscles, hardened by countless hours at the plow handles, at the machines.

Panting, cursing, locked in savage combat, they rolled across the road and into a ditch. Their bodies melded into the fantastic image of a four-legged, insanely violent creature.

In a last maniacal effort to ward off Leroy, Stan fired his gun twice in succession. The shots ricocheted off the asphalt roadbed.

Thrown into a frenzy by these shrill sounds of death, Leroy grabbed for the gun. Stan screamed hoarsely as the bone in his trigger finger snapped and the bullet cut into his chest.

Like a puppet whose strings have suddenly been cut, Stan fell back, crumpled. Utterly exhausted, Leroy fell on top of him, too beaten to make any attempt to rise.

In a quarter of an hour the manager and the two bouncers arrived on the scene.

"Let's clean up and be quick about it. Don't want the coppers here," the manager said. "Get a car."

Auto engines rumbled as the crowd from the gambling casino, sensing trouble and its attendant publicity, fled down the river line by a remote, river-bottom road twisting far away from the highway.

As the manager and his tough assistants were about to bundle Leroy and Stan into a car, the sheriff's car pulled up. Attracted by revolver shots on a routine cruise, they had come quickly to the scene.

Busy with the beginning of their investigation, the sheriff and his deputy did not notice when one of the bouncers stooped down to pick up a gun. The man picked it up with a handkerchief covering it and looked at the club owner for confirmation of his plan to drop it into the swamp.

The club owner shook his head and nodded toward Leroy, now beginning to recover slowly from the shock and fatigue of the fight with Stan.

Pretending to help him to his feet, the bouncer closed in on Leroy. With the touch of a professional pickpocket, he separated the flap on his jacket and dropped the gun in.

Nothing Leroy would say later in the trial could obliterate that single bit of damning "evidence."

And anyway, there wasn't much of a trial. The State had an open-and-shut case, and they shut Leroy away for twenty years.

CHAPTER THIRTEEN

FIRST there were tears, then fits of overwhelming depression, finally periods of abstinence, continence and a kind of all-inclusive self-deprivation. But nothing worked for Fran. Time and again the feeling persisted that nothing counted any more, that her life was, in a way, over—completely ruined. No sacrifice she made was harsh enough to make her truly atone for her cruelties and deceits. And other times no depth of abandon could drown out the memory of Stan's bloodied corpse, of Leroy rotting in jail. She rode the terror-filled highway of hell every day and night in her life for the first three months since the collapse of her new life as a high-living hellion.

Finally time itself created a sort of scar tissue. She began to throw off the nervous tensions of life lived alternately at the two extremes of indulgence or denial. As if her character was clay finally reshaping to its natural form after being subjected to rigors of heat and cold, Fran's basic nature reasserted itself. Life began not anew, but in the same manner and motivation as before—before Stan, Chunky, Leroy and the ugly degeneration of her plans for them. Stan had hidden Chunky's money and had died without telling her where. He truly died in vain.

If money had been important to Fran in the past, it was the core of her existence now. There was nothing else. Each of the men she'd been closely involved with—Stan, Leroy, Chunky—had come to a grisly end. Only money did not die; it could not die. Money could go on purchasing the silks and jewels and moments of physical pleasure; it endured, not prevailed (because it gave no warmth or comfort in the night that covered these silks and jewels from her sight), but made life bearable.

Fran did not save for that big trip to the Coast any more. She didn't want to fall in love with a man of her own choosing. The trip to the Coast was worthless; she would only have to live with herself there as well as here. And no man, no man now she knew, was alive who could give her happiness. She was a jinx to any man; and no man was worth anything to her. She hated them all.

This hate made her sane after her intervals of madness. At last, in hating Man as a basic, all-encompassing object of contempt, she was able to release, to divert some of the enormous pressure of hatred she had been directing inward, to herself.

Each new man she conned became her revenge on Stan for his bestiality, on Leroy and his wretched dependency, on Chunky and his degradation of her.

With the constancy of the stars and the tides, the pattern of her self-damnation imposed itself upon the daily actions of her life of destruction.

The warm autumn sunshine made Fran's skin glow. She had dashed quickly out of the payroll room when Power-Trak had issued its weekly paycheck, and had cashed it at once. It gave her a whole hour in which to make new contacts, to meet the new hillbillies up from Arkansas.

The men were in a laughing, happy-go-lucky mood. Like wild, irrepressible animals, they lived today as if there would be no tomorrow. All the streets of Power-Trak town glittered, it seemed, only to tempt them. And they did not resist temptation. They never had, never would with people like Sailor Sedlak ready to bully them, and luscious teases like Fran easily bulldozing them. But they didn't seem to mind at all, not, at least, until there just wasn't another odd two or three dollars *left* to meet another installment-purchase payment. Then they screamed and hollered and got into drunken trouble, until Fran—or one of her army of competitors—would come along and soothe them by offering them a spot cash loan "to tide them over," as the saying had it.

Fran walked back into the Power-Trak building and went to her locker. The men, she knew, would appreciate a bit of femininity in the middle of a dull, hot late September day. Accordingly, she put a dab of perfume under each earlobe and in the cleavage of her breasts.

"What was that oaf's name?" she said half to herself. She reached into her purse and extracted a neat little notebook, with a thumb index. Her experienced fingers quickly found the section of the notebook she was looking for.

WELHAUS, MERLE: 29, Arkansas dirt farmer, unmarried, fancies himself a ladies man; likes loud shirts and big, powerful cars. Not yet approached by Sailor Sedlak. Eats at southwest corner of the cafeteria.

After making a refresher check on the names of some ultra-generous local used-car dealers, Fran closed the book, stashed it in the locker and set out for the cafeteria.

The southwest corner of it, to be exact!

This one ain't much different from poor old Leroy, she thought to herself all the while her eyelashes batted in the unsuspecting fellow's direction. Same big, lovin' boy look in those dumb eyes. She got her food and moved toward her prey.

"Sure stays warm for September—almost October now," she said.

The Arky scraped a sliver of greasy pork chop out of a decayed molar with a dirty fingernail and said, "Hit shore does, Miss—Miss—"

"Oh, just call me Fran—Merle."

She leaned over close to him to make sure that the scent of her perfume would reach him.

"How in hell—excuse me for sayin' that—did you know me?"

"Oh, I hear the girls talkin' about you, and I said-well, the truth is I bet one of the girls that I would have the nerve to just come up right next to you and sit down and begin talking to you. We all—I mean I sure know *you*, Merle."

She giggled nervously.

"You mean *other* girls know about me? My gosh, some of the gals from back home must be up here spreading my good name, if you know what I mean?"

"Well, they do say you are all man, if you know what *I* mean?"

She tried the giggle again.

Merle laughed along with her.

In the background Fran could hear a couple of employees talking about her, watching her through suspicious, unfriendly eyes. "That's her, the flashy redhead. She's the one in that big murder case, helped send her boy friend up the river after he went and shot her husband," the taller of the two men said.

"Well, she'll get hers when he gets out, don't you worry about that. They all do," the other said, quietly, undressing her slowly in the eye of his mind.

" ... Yes, these evenings are warm, Merle. And I would sure like to go driving with you some evening after supper, Merle. What kind of a car do you drive? A '52 Chevy? Really? A Big Man like you? I sorta thought a '57 Olds 98 was more your style."

"It sure is my style, Fran. But I don't have that kind of money."

"You can spare ten dollars a week, can't you?"

"Yeah."

"Buy it on time, then. I know of a terrific buy. Wanta see it some night?"

"Maybe ... "

"Any time. But I sure was surprised to hear that you don't have a big, real impressive car like an Olds 98, Merle. You of all people—"

"Maybe we can go dancin' tonight and tomorrow night we can look at one," Merle said, his eyes scanning the full curve of her breasts straining against the light summer blouse.

"I'd like that—the dancin' with you, I mean," Fran said, letting her hand fall lightly to his knee in a gesture of what Merle took to be innocent, spontaneous affection.

She waited for him in that same old house of death. Sophie had gone off to another movie with Renie, but not before she warned her again about beginning the same old nasty business with the hicks. What Sophie didn't yet understand, Fran thought, was that there was nothing else left any more. She was like a hamster caught on a treadmill. There was nothing else to do, no need to be honest, no real pleasure in conning these suckers.

Somewhere in the house Stan had hidden the money. She was sure of that; it had to be here. He had no bank deposit books, no private safe deposit vault. So she lived in the house and searched it every day, every night she was home. It was like turning over a skeleton in its grave, she sometimes thought. But it had to be done. Not that she would do anything special with the money—just keep it, collect it—perhaps go on a fling one month, or a binge.

Three people suffered because of me, Fran thought. Two are dead, and one is just about dead in that prison. And no money. What did Stan do with the money?

Standing by the window she noticed Merle's battered car pull up. She watched him get out, throw back his shoulders and square his chin.

A man on the make, Fran thought, out to lay me, relay me, and parlay me.

Well, I just hope that idiot enjoys himself. Hah! It'll be for "free."

No sir, won't charge the lucky lad a cent; I'll just take it out in trade.

The dirty laugh she uttered stuck in her throat like a foul-tasting pellet of poison.

www.ingramcontent.com/pod-product-compliance
Lightning Source LLC
Chambersburg PA
CBHW052008240626
47153CB00008B/2787